THE PSALMS OF KING DAVID

Hope and Healing for Hard Times

by
Mark Baird

The Psalms of King David • Hope and Healing for Hard Times
Copyright © 2020 by Mark Baird

All rights reserved.

In accordance with the U.S. Copyright Act of 1976, no part of this publication may be reproduced, distributed, or transmitted in any form or by any means. The scanning, uploading, and electronic sharing of any part of this book without the permission of the publisher is unlawful piracy and theft of the author's intellectual property. If you would like to use material from this book (other than for review purposes), prior written permission must be obtained by contacting the publisher. Thank you for your support of the author's rights.

The Psalms of King David • Hope and Healing for Hard Times
Mark Baird

First Edition

Table of Contents

Introduction 5	Psalm 22 125
Psalm 1 9	Psalm 23 131
Psalm 2 15	Psalm 24 141
Psalm 3 21	Psalm 25 149
Psalm 4 25	Psalm 26 155
Psalm 5 31	Psalm 27 159
Psalm 6 39	Psalm 28 165
Psalm 7 43	Psalm 29 169
Psalm 8 49	Psalm 30 173
Psalm 9 55	Psalm 31 177
Psalm 10 63	Psalm 32 183
Psalm 11 67	Psalm 33 189
Psalm 12 75	Psalm 34 193
Psalm 13 79	Psalm 35 197
Psalm 14 81	Psalm 36 203
Psalm 15 89	Psalm 37 207
Psalm 16 95	Psalm 38 213
Psalm 17 101	Psalm 39 217
Psalm 18 105	Psalm 40 223
Psalm 19 111	Psalm 41 227
Psalm 20 115	A Study Guide 231
Psalm 21 119	About The Author 261

Introduction

The hope and healing that myriads across the millennia have discovered is found in a book written by one particular ancient prophet, King David of Judah, 2,700 years ago. In every circumstance the writer reveals his deep devotion and reliance upon God. Through David's deeply personal revelations in his psalms, we read of the emotions, struggles, fears, and defeats that we all experience. We find a kindred spirit, as he pleads for divine assistance in the midst of his hardships. And as David achieves victory over his destructive desires and afflictions, we discover how to do so too. The same faith and strength that King David possessed is available for us today. It is a faith that will enable us to endure during difficult times. We can have peace in the midst of turmoil. There is a lasting happiness available to us beyond anything offered on earth. We can stand securely when all else around us is falling down. – In the Book of Psalms, the God of Creation reveals to David, and to us, His divine plan for how we can live a life full of immense peace and bliss, despite any defeat or difficulty that life throws our way.

David is a marvelous example of resilient faith. His faith may sometimes bend, but it never breaks. Just as the keelson of a ship (the main beam that runs from stem to stern) holds a boat together, so David's trust in God and His promises were his strength that kept him from destruction. David pursued the Lord throughout his life. David was angered and grieved by enemies and the betrayal of friends, and weighed down by life's difficulties and tribulations, just as we have known too. But David persevered through his trials and tribulations and became victorious over them, because he continually turned to God for help.

David trusted the God of his ancestors. God had a plan and a purpose for David's life, just as He does for you and me. The Lord does not expect us to accomplish that plan by ourselves. Instead, God works within us to transform people into the image of His Son, Jesus Christ. The Lord does this for His purposes, for us to do the good deeds. ***"For we are God's handiwork, created in Christ Jesus to do good works, which God prepared in advance for us to do."*** (Ephesians 2:10)

Hardships, heartbreaks, loss, and sorrow are inevitable in this world. They can defeat us; or we can learn with God's help how to find peace in the midst of storms and respond to hatred with love. By thoughtfully reading the Psalms, we listen to God speaking to us. Gently and patiently, with tender loving care and forgiveness, God, by His words and His Spirit, seeks to change us into new people who are able to overcome temptations, trials, tribulations, and difficulties.

It is by trusting in the providential love of our Maker that we are able to please God and to be His children, walking in His light. We accomplish this by consuming the words of God every day. Just as bread and water nourishes our bodies, God's words nourish our hearts, minds, and souls. -- I have personally experienced this phenomenon over the course of my life's seven decades. My hope is that by reading these psalms you can see the hand of God's love, kindness, and mercy protecting, providing, and watching over you from the day your life began.

Ancient prophets who were divinely inspired foretold the hard times we all must endure in these days. They also foresaw a wonderful change occurring on earth! A new world is coming! A perfect Garden of Eden with no more death, wars, famines, diseases, and misery. God will be there. **"He will wipe away every tear from their eyes; and there will no longer be any death; there will no longer be any mourning, or crying, or pain; the first things have passed away."** (Revelation 21:4) -- My fervent hope is that all who read this book will be there with me! -- I hope that you will find countless new reasons to be grateful to our Maker, who cares for us with His unfathomable loving affection.

* * *

Textual Note: The Psalms are a compilation of worship songs that the Jews would sing in unison with a music director, musicians, and a choir. Only half of the psalms were written by David. The other Psalms were written by prophets and temple musicians after David's death, during and after the Jews exile to Babylon. All of these psalms were written in the days of the prophets, when God revealed great and wonderful things about their days and the "last days" in which we live today.

This book contains David's first book of Psalms. Four more books were added to the Psalms overtime, in which more of David's psalms were included. I have written books and study guides for those psalms too.

Note to Reader: Words in bold and *italicized* are direct quotes from each particular psalm. Words in bold but not **italicized** indicate passages from other parts of the Bible. The plain texts are my personal expositions. – Please read each psalm before reading my exposition. Although your bible may use different words, they will mean the same thing.

Psalm 1

In the first stanza, we are told what it means to be "***blessed***" by the Lord? That person ***"delights in the Lord."*** Is this not what we all seek, to be delighted and full of joy, to never have any worries, and to have our hearts flood with happy expectation every day? It is in the reading of God's words that we discover the myriad of blessings he bestows upon those who ***"plant themselves"*** by ***"the streams of living water"*** issuing forth from the Bible. It is those who feed upon God's words every day that are the blessed ones who ***"bear fruit."***

Jehovah, the boundless, ever-present, eternal, infinite, God, creator, and savior, who possesses all power, knows all things, who was, is, and forever will be, whose essential nature is righteousness, mercy, and love, divides all of humanity into two distinct groups: The Righteous and the Wicked. And throughout the Bible from Adam until today he has given us a choice: Life or Death. All must choose between living for God or living for themselves.

God is eternal and offers eternal life to those who ***"Do not walk in step with the wicked, or stand in the way that sinners take, or sit in the company of mockers."*** (verse 1) Mortal humans are not eternal. Those who oppose the ways of their creator and live for themselves rather than for Him will die and their spirits will live on in torment. How horrible for those who reject the love of God, versus the blessing of those who accept his free gift of forgiveness and eternal life. "***Therefore, the wicked will not stand in the judgment, nor sinners in the assembly of the righteous. For the LORD watches over the way of the righteous, but the way of the wicked leads to destruction.***" (verses 5–6)

Jesus, the Son in the Trinity, God in human flesh, says "**Those that abide and remain in me, will bear much fruit.**" (John 15:5) But He says to those who refuse to do so, "**If you do not remain in me, you are like a branch that is thrown away and withers; such branches are picked up, thrown into the fire and burned.**" (John 15:6) Then he reiterates and concludes with, "**This is to my Father's glory, that you bear much fruit, showing yourselves to be my disciples.**" (John 15:8)

The choice seems obvious and simple; yet, the majority of humanity rejects Jesus Christ, God stepping down from His throne in heaven to take on human flesh, and to reveal his love for us. Instead, most people live however they choose, without any concern for the eternal consequences. But those that seek the Lord with all their heart, and ask him to fill them with the passion, wisdom, peace, and joy of God's Holy Spirit, recognize the voice of God's Spirit as they read his holy words. They drink from it as trees do from water. Such persons will "***not wither.***" Whatever they put their hands to do "***will prosper.***" (verse 3)

"***Their leaf does not wither***" is a call for Christians to be resilient. We "***yield fruit* in *season.***" Life has many seasons. Not all the days of a Christian's life are rosy. Rain must fall. Storms come to bring forth a harvest. We all have our late Fall and long Winters. But Jesus says to not allow the green of our faith's leaves to wither.

Jesus declared, "**I am the true Vine, and My Father is the vinedresser. Every branch in Me that does not bear fruit, He takes away; and every branch that continues to bear fruit, He prunes, so that it will bear more fruit.**" (John 15:1–2) If we choose to believe this, the Lord gives us this promise: "**These things I have spoken to you so that My joy may be in you, and that your joy may be made full.**" (John 15:11) The choice seems obvious and simple. It requires us to do a few things: remaining, abiding, and resting in our faith in God.

It is not enough to give your heart to Jesus for a while. This is a daily and conscious choice we make every day, all day long. Coming to Jesus is a lifetime commitment. He warns us repeatedly to endure in our faith, and to walk along the 'straight and narrow' *road*. We are not to leave that path by turning to the right or to the left. "**Because strait is the gate, and narrow is the way which leadeth unto life, and few there be that find it.**" (Matt. 17:14)

Jesus gives those who persevere in their faith and "**endure until the end,**" wonderful promises in the 2nd and 3rd chapters of Revelation. This is one of the blessings promised, "**I will also keep you from the hour of trial that is going to come on the whole world.**" (Revelation 3:10) This verse refers to the last 7 years on earth, the "Tribulation." Jesus warns us that this will be the most horrific time on earth, and the end of this edition of earth and those that oppose God. Jesus promises to keep us from "**that hour.**" It is one of the most wonderful promises in the Bible. This event is when the Lord descends to the clouds and calls all those that died in Christ, and all that are alive who are faithful, to rise up and receive their new, eternal bodies. **"Listen, I tell you a mystery: We will not all sleep, but we will all be changed in a flash, in the twinkling of an eye, at the last trumpet. For the trumpet will sound, the dead will be raised imperishable, and we will be changed. For the perishable must clothe itself with the imperishable, and the mortal with immortality. When the perishable has been clothed with the imperishable, and the mortal with immortality, then the saying that is written will come true: "Death has been swallowed up in victory." -- For the Lord himself shall descend from heaven with a shout, with the voice of the archangel, and with the trump of God: and the dead in Christ shall rise first: Then we which are alive and remain shall be caught up together with them in the clouds, to meet the Lord in the air: and so shall we ever be with the Lord."** (1 Corinthians 15:51–57)

Those who do not believe that Jesus is God's Son and our savior, or who fall away from the faith, this severe warning is directed: They will miss the escape from earth before the Tribulation. These must experience the horrors of God's wrath poured out upon an unbelieving and wicked world. Jesus warns us: **"Remember therefore how thou hast received and heard, and hold fast, and repent. If therefore thou shalt not watch,**

I will come on thee as a thief, and thou shalt not know what hour I will come upon thee." (Revelation 3:3)

All who believe the words of this following scripture, which speak of the Messiah, Jesus Christ, who died for our sins and rose from the dead so that we might rise from death too, will receive eternal life. "**In the beginning was the Word, and the Word was with God, and the Word was God. He was with God in the beginning. Through him all things were made; without him nothing was made that has been made. In him was life, and that life was the light of all mankind… He came to that which was his own, but his own did not receive him. Yet to all who did receive him, to those who believed in his name, he gave the right to become children of God— children born not of natural descent, nor of human decision, or a husband's will, but born of God. The Word became flesh and made his dwelling among us. We have seen his glory, the glory of the one and only Son, who came from the Father, full of grace and truth.**" (John 1: 1-4, 10-14)

If we abide in Jesus Christ, then we will overcome. We will be granted this greatest gift in the universe: "**To him that endures until the end will I grant to sit with me in my throne, even as I also overcame, and am set down with my Father in his throne.**" (Rev. 3:21)

It would be cruel of the Lord to give us these warnings and great promises without telling us how to remain faithful. The answer to how we accomplish this great task of our lives, remaining true to God and to living according to his will, is in the second verse of the first Psalm: "***Delight is in the law of the LORD,***

meditate on his law day and night." (verse 2)Consider the Bible as important as the sun, soil, and water are to trees. Just as plants and trees cannot bloom and bear flowers and fruit without it, our hearts, souls, and minds cannot be nourished unless we drink from the well of God's words and nourish our souls every day. Thus, let us learn the conclusion of Psalm 1 and never forget. Choose "***the way of the righteous***" and live! "***For the LORD watches over the way of the righteous, but the way of the wicked leads to destruction.***" (verse 6)

Psalm 2

In the first verses we are asked the question that all the saints and the angels in heaven have pondered: Why does humanity hate God? *"Why do the nations rage, and the peoples meditate a vain thing? The kings of the earth set themselves, and the rulers take counsel together, against Jehovah, and against his anointed, saying "Let us break their bonds asunder and cast away their cords from us."* (verses 1-4)

Before the rebellion of Adam and Eve, they lived in perfect harmony with their Creator, who walked and talked with them at dusk each day. They had sweet fellowship together. As the caretakers of the Garden, they had the free choice and the liberty to do whatever they wanted, except for one rule: **"And the LORD God commanded the man, "You are free to eat from any tree in the garden; but you must not eat from the tree of the knowledge of good and evil, for when you eat from it you will certainly die."** (Genesis 2:17)

Even in this perfect state of oneness with God, when Satan suggested that God was not as loving, truthful, and as gracious as He claimed, Adam and Eve turned away from trusting in their loving Creator and believed and obeyed the Serpent

(Satan). He encouraged them to eat of the forbidden tree, saying, **"God knows that when you eat from it your eyes will be opened, and you will be like God, knowing good and evil."** (Genesis 3:5) They were tempted with the same abominable desire as Satan had committed when he led a rebellion to overcome Christ and to sit on his throne: Pride and Greed. Their hearts had turned from wanting to please God, to coveting his authority. **"When the woman saw that the fruit of the tree was good for food and pleasing to the eye, and also desirable for gaining wisdom, she took some and ate it. She also gave some to her husband, who was with her, and he ate it."** (Genesis 3:6) – Mankind is a ravenous beast. His cravings are never satisfied. We covet what we do not have. **"You desire but do not have, so you kill. You covet but you cannot get what you want, so you quarrel and fight. You do not have because you do not ask God."** (James 4:2)

Oh, for the patience to wait and to ask and hear from God. What would have happened if they waited until the cool evening, when God came to talk with them? But our impulse is to grasp what we desire whenever we can. By the power of the free will God gave to them, they used it to rebel against his authority. **"Then the eyes of both of them were opened, and they realized they were naked; so, they sewed fig leaves together and made coverings for themselves."** (Genesis 3:7) -- May the Lord open our eyes to see and to root out the sin lurking within us. The greatest wisdom for all mankind to possess in this: **"Trust in the LORD with all your heart and lean not on your own understanding; in all your ways submit to him, and he will make your paths straight."** (Proverbs 3:3-6)

Certainly, after God cast them out of his garden Adam and Eve were consumed with regret and remonstrated themselves for the foolish sin they committed.

Ever since the first sin, there have been an uncountable number of other sins. The earth is saturated in them. Mankind has never ceased to seek his freedom from the authority of their Creator. "*He that sitteth in the heavens will laugh: The Lord will have them in derision. Then will he speak unto them in his wrath and vex them in his sore displeasure.*" (verses 4-5) This is a promise for a day of judgement for mankind. God in his unfathomable mercy has waited since that day in the Garden to bring his elect and his chosen back into a perfect relationship again. Those that continue to refuse to honor God will receive eternal dishonor. Those who comply and submit themselves to the will and the way of life prescribed by our Creator will live in great honor with the Lord of heaven and earth forever.

God sent his Son, the exact representation of our Father in heaven, to reveal to the world the heart of God. Jesus healed the sick, the blind, the lame. He associated with the downtrodden and the despised. Jesus obeyed the Father's will even to dying on a cross to pay the penalty of all of mankind's sins. He did so that we might understand the greatness of The Father's love for us; for, "**The Lord is longsuffering to you, not wishing that any should perish, but that all should come to repentance.**" (2 Peter 3:9)

The God-man, Jesus has been appointed as the earth's king. He will rule over a new earth forever, in righteous, justice and love.

"Yet I have set my king upon my holy hill of Zion. I will tell of the decree: Jehovah said unto me, Thou art my son; this day have I begotten thee. Ask of me, and I will give thee the nations for thine inheritance, and the uttermost parts of the earth for thy possession. Thou shalt break them with a rod of iron; thou shalt dash them in pieces like a potter's vessel. Now therefore be wise, O ye kings: Be instructed, ye judges of the earth. Serve Jehovah with fear and rejoice with trembling. Kiss the Son, lest he be angry, and ye perish in the way, for his wrath will soon be kindled. Blessed are all they that take refuge in him." (verses 6-12)

The apostle John begins his recounting of his time with Jesus and his teaching and miracles by telling us who the man Jesus Christ really is: "**In the beginning was the Word, and the Word was with God, and the Word was God. He was with God in the beginning. Through him all things were made; without him nothing was made that has been made.**" (John 1:1-3) John refers to Jesus as the creator of all things and claims that Jesus is God. Furthermore, he writes this: "**The Word became flesh and made his dwelling among us. We have seen his glory, the glory of the one and only Son, who came from the Father, full of grace and truth.**" (John 1:14) John the Baptist also claimed this of Jesus: "**No one has ever seen God, but the one and only Son, who is himself God and is in closest relationship with the Father, has made him known.**" (John 1:9)

John the Apostle wrote this most famous of Jesus' quotations: "**For God so loved the world that he gave his one and only

Son, that whoever believes in him shall not perish but have eternal life. For God did not send his Son into the world to condemn the world, but to save the world through him. Whoever believes in him is not condemned..." (John 3:16-17) But 800 years before that was said, David, a great king and an anointed prophet wrote at the end of Psalm 2: *"**Kiss the Son, lest he be angry, and ye perish in the way, for his wrath will soon be kindled. Blessed are all they that take refuge in him.**"* (verse 12) This was already known by David through the timeless wisdom of the Holy Spirit of God.

The Son of God, Jesus Christ, boldly claimed this "**I am the way, the truth, and the source of all life. No one can come to the Father and receive eternal life apart from me.**" (John 14:6) Our primary goal in our lives is to glorify the Son of God. He loves us so much that he willingly suffered and died in our place. He died so that we can live! Then he rose from his grave and ascended to heaven. -- So too will those that *"**take refuge in Him**."* (verse 12)

Psalm 3

This Psalm was written when David's son, Absalom, tried to usurp his father's throne. Think of the triple dose of pain David experienced. His son has raised an army, which includes David's trusted friends. Absalom is marching upon Jerusalem; David's kingdom and his people are being threatened. **"LORD, how many are my foes! How many revolt against me! Many are saying of me, "God will not deliver him."** (verses 1-2)

David had already lost two sons before. The first was the child of his adulterous affair with Bathsheba. That baby died within a week. David had prayed fervently for God to spare the life of that child; but his sin was too great. The baby died. When David heard this, he rose and ate. When he regained his composure, with subdued sorrow, he said, **"Someday, I will go to be with him, since he can no longer be with me."** (2 Samuel 12:23) He knew with certainty that there is a life after death for the innocent and the righteous. He knew that his baby was not lost forever. By this faith, he consoled himself.

David lost another son when Absalom was an adult. In revenge for his sister's rape by a half-brother, Amnon, Absalom murdered him and fled to another country. After a few years, by the urging of an advisor, David promised Absalom safety if he returned to Judah. But David did not see nor welcome Absalom when he returned. There was no reconciliation.

Perhaps Absalom was angry at his father for not punishing Amnon for raping his sister, Tamar, and having to take revenge himself. Absalom was very handsome the scriptures say. And he had a charismatic personality. He used these attributes to foster a rebellion led by some of David's advisors, military officers, and trusted friends.

Before the battle between the armies of Absalom and his father, David went to the Mount of Olives, where Jesus would pray before his crucifixion. This Psalm is a like that prayer. How often do we lay down at night full of anxiety? But probably none of us have faced an army raised by our own son! So, David fled from the city with those that had remained faithful to him. Now, he was exhausted and laid down to sleep. ***"I lie down and sleep; I wake again, because the LORD sustains me."*** (verse 5)

Most people would not be able to sleep under these circumstances. We would probably keep running as far away from this threat as we could until we dropped. But David had faced many enemies who were mightier in strength and defeated them with the help of his God. So, he consoles and calms his fears before closing his eyes. He is comforted with his faith: ***"LORD, you are a shield around me, my glory, the One who lifts my head high."*** (verse 3) What confidence! His assurance of God's call upon his life and the promises made to David about his rule were a rock beneath the king's feet. ***"I will not fear though tens of thousands assail me on every side."*** (verse 6)

And David did not finish his prayer and fall into slumber until he also prays for those for whom he is responsible to keep safe: "**From the LORD comes deliverance. May your blessing be on your people.**" (verse 8) Whenever we suffer and pray, we should remember to pray for those believers who may be suffering from the same dilemma. Never think only of only ourselves when we come before God. We are all members of the same body of Christ. If we suffer, remember to ask for our fellow brothers and sisters who need prayer too.

The next day, David and his much smaller army defeated Absalom and his army. But despite David's strict orders not to harm Absalom, one of David's generals, perhaps made the wiser decision. He made sure that the rebellion ended. He slew Absalom. And down through the ages we still hear David's cry of lament when he heard that news: "**O my son, Absalom, my son, my son Absalom! Would I had died for you, O Absalom, my son, my son!**" (2 Samuel 18:33) -- We did not hear this cry after the death of David's baby by Bathsheba. Why? Because David knew that child was in heaven. Not so with Absalom. His fate is sealed. David will not see this son ever again!

Some of our dearly loved ones have refused to believe. They may not even listen to our pleas to heed God's word. This is the deepest pain of all when those die. So, while we have the opportunity, let us make the best use of our time with those we dearly love. There is nothing more important in all the world for them to know than Jesus is Lord, and that Jesus loves and forgives them. If they will receive Him into their hearts as their God and Savior, like we have, they will be forgiven and freely receive God's gift of eternal life!

Psalm 4

David begins with: *"Answer me when I call to you, my righteous God. Give me relief from my distress; have mercy on me and hear my prayer."* (verse 1) David is not pleading with his Maker; but he addresses Jehovah with certainty. David is saying this: *"I know that you will answer me, my righteous God. You have always heard me and relieved me when I am in distress. And I know that because of your mercy, you will hear me and give me relief again."* – David confirms this meaning when, after pleading for his people to repent, he says: *"Know that the LORD has set apart his faithful servant for himself; the LORD hears when I call to him."* (verse 3)

"Offer the sacrifices of the righteous and trust in the LORD." (verse 4) Much of our faith is based on our own personal experiences with the One and Only God, Jehovah. It was vital for Israel, and it still is for believers today, to celebrate and remember the miraculous deliverances and deeds of Jehovah. David continually recites them as proof of God's overseeing love for his people.

"Fill my heart with joy." (verse 7) David had experienced many miraculous interventions in his life. When he was a boy

shepherd, a lion attacked his sheep, and another time a bear. But the small boy, alone in the wilderness with the sheep he was to protect and care for, did not run. David had confidence in the Lord. He was the shepherd. His job was to defend his sheep. So, he killed the lion and the bear with his own hands. Afterwards, we read of his valor and defeat of the giant Goliath. – David's confidence in God made him stand head and shoulders above all other men, despite his stature, even above giants. He was made King and was victorious in battles. David also acquired tremendous riches of gold, silver, bronze, jewels, and timber. He stored these to be used for the building of God's temple by his son Solomon.

Even though, in David's life and in ours, we will have seasons of trial. It may be because of sin; or it may be the love of God reaching deeper into our hearts to grow our trust and faith in Him. During these stretches when it seems as though our prayers are not heard, and that our God is silent to our pleading, we must proclaim as did David: "*I know that the LORD has set apart his faithful servant for himself; the LORD hears when I call to him.*" (verse 3) We should never trust our emotions to lead us in the path of truth and peace. We must stand upon our past and personal experiences of answered prayer and blessings, and upon the truth in God's word, the Bible.

Notice for whom David is pleading. It is not for himself; but, for his people, the sheep of his pasture. As their King, he was also their Shepherd. When he cries out to God, in distress he says, "*How long will you people turn my glory into shame? How long will you love delusions and seek false gods?*" (verse

2) The king and shepherd's heart was broken because of the sins of his people.

David contrasts our two main choices in life throughout the Psalms, the blessings of walking in the ways of the Lord, and the consequences of those that do not. Everywhere in the Bible we are asked to make those critical choices. Moses asked the people that God gave him to shepherd to make that choice, which David has also urged his people to make. The message of this Psalm is much like to what Moses exhorted his people. **"See, I set before you today life and prosperity, death and destruction. For I command you today to love the LORD your God, to walk in obedience to him, and to keep his commands, decrees and laws; then you will live and increase, and the LORD your God will bless you in the land you are entering to possess. But if your heart turns away and you are not obedient, and if you are drawn away to bow down to other gods and worship them, I declare to you this day that you will certainly be destroyed… This day I call the heavens and the earth as witnesses against you that I have set before you life and death, blessings, and curses. Now choose life, so that you and your children may live and that you may love the LORD your God, listen to his voice, and hold fast to him."** (Deuteronomy 30:15-20)

Many of the false gods back then, and still today, are "gods of prosperity." In ancient times and throughout history until today, people do many things to appease the god of this world in efforts to gain more worldly goods. Even in some 'Christian" churches the "Prosperity Gospel," is preached. They entice their trusting congregations away from the things of the Spirit and draw them into worshipping the things of this world. Christians are "**not of this world,**" (John 15:19), just as our Savior. We should never seek to be rich in the things of this world. Instead, we are to "***Offer the sacrifices of the righteous and trust in the LORD.***" (Psalm 4:5) That is how we open the door to receiving God's riches. Repentance, turning away from sinful behavior and turning towards God, is always the first step to knowing and receiving from Christ. It is the only real path to finding "**everlasting joy unspeakable, and full of glory.**" (1 Peter 1:8)

Why are David's people going after false gods? For the same reason, all humanity does: "***Many, LORD, are asking, "Who will bring us prosperity?"***" (verse 6) We are instructed throughout the Bible to be content with what the Lord provides us: The Apostle Paul exhorts us to be like he is: "**I have learned to be content in all circumstances. I know what it is to be in need, and I know what it is to have plenty. I have learned the secret of being content in any and every situation, whether well fed or hungry, whether living in plenty or in want. I can do all this through him who gives me strength.**" (Philippians 4:11-13)

According to Strong's *Complete Concordance of the Bible*, ***shalom*** means "*completeness, soundness, and welfare.*" It represents completeness in number and safety and soundness in our physical body. ***Shalom*** also covers our relationship with God. This is why the Apostle Paul, a former Jewish teacher of the law, says this. "**Be anxious for nothing, but in everything by**

prayer and supplication with thanksgiving let your requests be made known to God. And the peace (Shalom) **of God, which surpasses all comprehension, will guard your hearts and your minds in Christ Jesus."** (Philippians 4:6-7)

The prosperity of the world is NOT the same as the prosperity that God offers us. Jehovah offers us a peace and prosperity that is "**not of this world.**" It is far better because it lasts forever. It is our assurance that we are *"set apart"* as God's beloved children; and that we have a wonderful future that He has prepared for us. Therefore, David gives precise but simple directions as an exhortation to his wayward people: *"**Know that the LORD has set apart his faithful servant for himself; the LORD hears when I call to him. Tremble and do not sin; when you are on your beds, search your hearts and be silent. Offer the sacrifices of the righteous and trust in the LORD.**"* (verses 3-4)

On his "Sermon on the Mount," Jesus reiterated Moses' and David's directions: **"Therefore I tell you, do not be anxious about your life, what you will eat, nor about your body, what you will put on. . . . For your Father knows that you need them. Instead, seek his kingdom, and these things will be added to you."** (Matthew 6:25-34)

It is a gross error to use the world's definition of "prosperity" when reading about the fullness of God's riches that we have received through our faith in God's Son, Jesus the Messiah. David and Paul desired the same thing for their people. Their goal was: **"My goal is that they may be encouraged in heart and united in love, so that you may have the full riches of complete understanding, in order that you may know the**

mystery of God, namely, Christ, in whom are hidden all the treasures of wisdom and knowledge." (Colossians 2:2) Jesus is our Shalom and treasure: peace and prosperity. Thus, David concludes the 4th Psalm with: "***In peace*** (Shalom) ***I will lie down and sleep, for you alone, LORD, make me dwell in safety.***" (verse 8)

A 19th century evangelist summed up this psalm with: "*I know that my God and Father will hear me when I call to him in Jesus' name. Jesus is my hope and my righteousness. Henceforth, I will lay me down to sleep securely in Jesus, accepted as his beloved; for this is the rest wherewith the Lord gives to the weary, and this is his refreshing.*" (Charles Spurgeon)

Psalm 5

David begins where we all begin in bringing our petitions before God, "*Give ear to my words, O LORD, consider my groaning. Heed the sound of my cry for help, my King and my God; for, to You I pray.*" (verses 1-2) -- David is not pleading for God to hear his prayers. He is confident that God always does. But he is desperate, and so his prayer is urgent. He has become overwhelmed by the conspiracies, and secret assaults upon his character, by those who merely pretend to be his friends: those who are always flattering David and then speaking cruelly and untruthfully about him behind his back. He describes the kind of people God hates. "*For you are not a God who is pleased with wickedness; with you, evil people are not welcome. The arrogant cannot stand in your presence. You hate all who do wrong; you destroy those who tell lies. The bloodthirsty and deceitful you, Lord, detest.*" (verses 4-6)

Throughout the Bible we are told of God's anger, hatred, and vengeance against his enemies, those who refuse to follow the innate sense of right and wrong that the Lord has put into the hearts of all mankind. David prays for God to judge them and to "*destroy*" them. – How can we pray what David does when Christ has commanded us to forgive our enemies and to pray for them to receive the same grace and mercy we have a received? God is the Judge, not ourselves. So, let us with Jesus have this in our hearts, "**I have come as Light into the world, so that everyone who believes in Me will not remain in darkness. If anyone hears My sayings and does not keep them, I do not judge him; for I did not come to judge the world, but to save the world. He who rejects Me and does not receive My sayings, has one who judges him; the word I spoke is what will judge him at the last day.**" (John 12:46-47)

The Apostle John describes why believers and unbelievers cannot have intimate fellowship together: "**This is the message we have heard from him and declare to you: God is light; in him there is no darkness at all.**" (John 1:5) This is an unchangeable truth. Light and darkness cannot share the same space anywhere in the universe. Light always banishes darkness. We all know that when we flip a switch to turn on the house lights that it makes the darkness go away. They are inherent enemies. And just as there is this immutable law of the physical universe, so it also true of the spiritual cosmos.

Christians are God's army on earth. We have chosen which side we will serve. We serve the one and only Creator of all, who is perfect in everything he does. Our God is flawless. He is pure holiness and light. And such are we to be too. Therefore, he gives us "**armor**" to defend ourselves and a sword (the truth of God's word) to conquer and become victorious over our sins and defects.

Those that refuse to believe in their Creator, the God who loves them and blesses them every day, have chosen their side. They battle on the side of darkness, regardless of how deceived and ignorant they may be. Just as Satan deceived a third of God's angels in heaven to rebel against God's authority over them, so many more humans have also followed after the enticements of Satan and this world, which he rules over until Christ returns as the true and righteous ruler of the earth and all mankind.

Therefore, when we read of David's hatred for those who practice evil, understand that he is feeling what God feels. But David takes comfort in knowing that they will not persist in their persecutions, oppressions and lying, because there is a Judge in heaven, who will someday deliver them to the punishment they deserve. With Satan and his rebellious angels, people who persist in evil and refuse to repent, will also be cast into the **"Lake of Fire," which is the second death."** (Revelation 20:14) Their souls will live on with the everlasting grief for their foolishness because they choose the path of rebellion. However, if they repent before they die, in heartfelt sincerity, and call upon Jesus to forgive them, they will inherit the eternal blessings of God. The atoning blood of Christ washes away all of our sins.

All true believers wait patiently, and endure many sorrows and afflictions, just as Christ also did, by the hands and schemes of evil people. We understand when David cries out against our enemies: "***By their own devices let them fall! In the multitude of their transgressions thrust them out; for, they are rebellious against You.***" (verse 10)

It is perfectly holy for Christians to hate evil. But how should we feel about those that practice it? They rob, steal, and lie. They oppress the poor, the widow, the orphan. They fill the earth with perversions and evil. They murder, rape, and create havoc. They are merciless, and their thoughts are continually opposed to God. They refuse to believe in what He says. They do not take Him seriously. And so, they can do all kinds of evil; for, they have hardened their hearts to listening to His Truth.

God rejects evil in all its forms and disguises. He hates the harm that the godless do to themselves, others, and even to our earth. – We can also experience this righteous anger of God's since He lives within us. -- And yet, just as Jesus preached until the end, and even saved an evil man next to Him while he hung on his cross, so we are to persist in preaching and being living examples of God's grace and forgiveness until we take our last breath.

In the Old Testament, God's people were to eradicate all unbelieving tribes within the land God had given to them. But in the New Testament, Christians are to show mercy and to **"Love your enemies and pray for those that persecute you that you may be sons of your Father in heaven. He causes His sun to rise on the evil and the good and sends rain on the righteous and the unrighteous..."** (Matthew 5:44). And again: **"Show proper respect to everyone, love the family of believers, fear God, honor your leaders."** (1 Peter 2:17)

With this understanding, let us move on into the richness of God's words. Whenever we read about God's hatred of his enemies, and the enemies who mistreat and slander us, God reminds us that there is a day set for judgement of all wickedness practiced by unbelievers. But until that day, treat all men with respect, as also made in the image of God. Preach the Gospel in love. Warn them of their impending doom. Offer them the way of escape from this judgement that is to come. Let them know what Christ did for them when he died and rose from the dead, the first of a multitude of those who will rise in like manner. "**And this is love: that we walk in obedience to his commands. As you have heard from the beginning, his command is that you walk in love.**" (2 John:6)

"Heed the sound of my cry for help, my King and my God, for to You I pray. In the morning, O LORD, you will hear my voice; In the morning I will order my prayer to You and eagerly watch. For You are not a God who takes pleasure in wickedness; no evil dwells with You." (verses 2-3) -- David knows that God hears him when he prays. In fact, the Bible teaches us that God hears every thought we think, sees all our dreams, hears every word we speak, and knows what we are going to do before we do it. Everything is recorded in God's book. He sees all. He knows all. But to his "beloved" he pays special attention, just as we do for our own children. God always listens when we speak to him. He cares about us. He provides and protects us. He has put a plan in our hearts for us to follow in our lives. All of our sinful deeds have been erased from His book. "**He remembers them no more!**" (Isaiah 43:25) For that we should always be thankful, every minute of every day. it is our source of constant joy!

This is how Jesus answered when he was asked how to enter into the kingdom of God by a young rich man: "**You shall love the**

Lord your God with all your heart, and with all your soul, and with all your strength, and with all your mind'; and 'Your neighbor as yourself." (Luke 10:27)– When we begin every day by coming before the Lord in reverence, thanksgiving, and praise, we enter into his personal, and holy presence. **"Enter into his gates with thanksgiving, and into his courts with praise; be thankful unto him and bless his name. For the LORD is good; his mercy is everlasting; and his truth endures to all generations."** (Psalm 100:4-5)

We must make time for the Lord, every day and night, regardless of our endless duties during the day, and our fatigue in the evening. For when we bring our burdens and griefs and needs before our God, we have the excitement and expectancy of his reply. As David says, we begin then to "***eagerly* watch**." (verse 3) God always answers our prayers, especially those that we make with faith in his promises: a faith that expects God to answer.

Why must we do this every day? "***For you are not a God who takes pleasure in wickedness; no evil dwells with You. The boastful shall not stand before Your eyes; You hate all who do iniquity.***" (verses 4-5) This speaks of mankind's fallen nature that has resulted in afflicting humanity with a desire to rebel against God's rule. Like Adam and Eve, we want to "*be like God*" and make our own decisions. That is why it is critical for David and for us to make a sacrifice of time at the start and end of our days and nights. After waking, come humbly and gratefully into God's Holy Presence. When we do, He clothes us with the gifts of armor that God has made for us to defend us from evil. "**Stand therefore, having girded your waist with truth, having put on the breastplate of righteousness, and having shod your feet with the preparation of the gospel of peace; above all, taking the shield of faith with which, you will be able to quench all the fiery darts of the wicked one. And take the helmet of salvation, and the sword of the Spirit, which is the word of God; praying always with all prayer and supplication in the Spirit …**" (Ephesians 6:14-18).

For us to walk on the straight and narrow Road of Righteousness, and to avoid becoming the kind of person God will judge, we must take the time to bow in reverence and prayer. *"By Your abundant lovingkindness I will enter Your house, at Your holy temple I will bow in reverence for You. O LORD, lead me in Your righteousness because of my foes; make Your way straight before me."* (verse 7-8)

David then reiterates again his prayer for all believers. He closes with: *"But let all who take refuge in You be glad. Let them ever sing for joy. And may You shelter them, that those who love Your name may exult in You. For it is You who blesses the righteous man, O LORD, you surround him with favor as with a shield."* (verses 11-12)

King David prayed every day and continued in that Spirit until he laid down to sleep. We are encouraged to do the same. We must if we desire to be surrounded with *God's favor*.

Psalm 6

In our life we will not avoid an experience like what David expresses here: *"**My soul is in deep anguish. How long, LORD, how long?**"* (verse 4) God has turned away from David in His anger and chastisement of him. However, as David continues in prayer before the Lord, his attitude changes. David concludes this Psalm with, *"**Away from me, all you who do evil, for the LORD has heard my weeping. The LORD has heard my cry for mercy; the LORD accepts my prayer. All my enemies will be overwhelmed with shame and anguish; they will turn back and suddenly be put to shame.**"* (verses 9-10)

As so often happened to David in his life, also happens to us: When we are sick or suffering emotionally, financially, relationship-wise, etc. we often jump to the conclusion that perhaps God is angry at us, or punishing us. We turn in our beds, wet with tears, grief, and pain, towards our Savior who calls us his "Beloved," and accuse him of being the cause of what we are experiencing. But if we have no conviction of sin; if the Holy Spirit is not revealing to us anything that we did to cause God to be angry, do not jump to that conclusion. When we are very sorely afflicted, and have grown weak, and a cure seems hopeless, depression follows it. We look up towards Heaven and ask God the same question: "***How much longer before you heal me?***" (verse 3) Like David, we also pray to be restored to spiritual, mental, physical, and emotional health.

In this Psalm is a condition that we all too often encounter in this world: Those we love and trust turn on us. Their true feeling for us and their secret intentions are revealed. Throughout the Psalms we hear David crying and despondent because those he thought loved him, did not. Unfaithfulness is possibly the greatest pain humans and their Creator encounter. "***Away from me, all you who do evil, for the LORD has heard my weeping.***" (verse 8)

Believers are God's beloved children, his friends, and even his brothers and sisters. He loves us with a love far too great for any human to imagine! Yes, he promises to chastise us. That just means that as any loving father, he will discipline us and teach us right from wrong. But never listen, nor submit to the accusations of those who insist that your suffering means that God no longer loves you because of your struggles. The Bible repeats over and over in many ways this certain knowledge that we must all grasp throughout our lives: God loves us so much for believing in His Son's great sacrifice and resurrection; we need never be frightened of Him any longer.

Contrast the despondency of David's misery with the joyous elation in Psalm 103: "**The LORD is compassionate and gracious, slow to anger, abounding in love. He will not always accuse, nor will he harbor his anger forever. He does not treat us as our sins deserve or repay us according to our**

iniquities. For as high as the heavens are above the earth, so great is his love for those who fear him; as far as the east is from the west, so far has he removed our transgressions from us. As a father has compassion on his children, so the LORD has compassion on those who fear him." (Psalm 103:8-14) Who else but God can possibly help us the most in our afflictions? We cannot control what others choose to do. And quite often we will not comprehend why they can be so cruel. Those we love can also hurt us to the very marrow of our bones. How many of us can identify with what David was feeling: *"even my bones are in agony."* (verse 2)

Jesus made many wonderful promises to us. But he also often warned us: **"I have told you these things, so that in me you may have peace. In this world you will have trouble. But take heart! I have overcome the world."** (John 16:33) In the Gospel of Matthew Jesus continues and encourages us: **"But the one who perseveres until the end will be saved."** (Matthew 24:13)

David concludes his Psalm: *"**The LORD has heard my cry for mercy; the LORD accepts my prayer. All my enemies will be overwhelmed with shame and anguish; they will turn back and suddenly be put to shame.**"* (verse 10)

Dear brothers and sisters in Christ, fellow saints, throughout the brief time mankind has been on earth, we all have suffered and endured; but, as Jesus encourages us, when we go through such trials, we are to strengthen our hearts and hope in the Lord's mercy. Let us put our hope in and find strength in God and in his precious words.

We have all heard: "*Bad things happen to good people, and good things happen to bad people.*" This was also a constant saying that David and the prophets pondered. The Bible actually makes it quite clear that faith in Jesus Christ does not guarantee a good life, but a perfect eternity. Indeed, there are more predictions in Scripture of a struggle on earth for the believer before our Lord's return than there is of gain and success." Our brief time on earth has one primary purpose: We are to choose between believing and trusting in the one and only true God, Jehovah, or not to believe. And those that profess their faith in Jehovah are tested. Their faith is tried as in a furnace that removes the dross from precious metals.

June Hunt, a beautiful Christian writer wrote, "*In both the Old and New Testaments, we find numerous references to the refining of gold and silver as a parallel of God's refining us through painful trials. This is meant to help us understand the purpose beyond our pain—to conform us to the character of Christ. Clearly, we do not develop Christlike character all at once. Character is forged over time, especially through fiery trials. Indeed, God is our Refiner.*" -- "**God tests us; He refines us like silver**." (Psalm 66:10)

Psalm 7

Psalm 7 is a desperate plea for deliverance from an enemy too strong for David to defeat, at least alone. So, he does what all believers in Jehovah do when in danger; he runs straight into our Lord's willing and loving arms to find refuge (a place of peace, comfort, and safety). This is a continual theme throughout the Psalms and all the books of the Bible. **"But let all who take refuge in you rejoice; let them sing joyful praises forever. Spread your protection over them, that all who love your name may be filled with joy."** (Psalm 5:11)Perhaps like myself, you have experienced this cry when your child falls and think they have hurt themselves, "Daddy! Daddy!" I distinctly recall hearing this when my daughter was 5 and fell down our rugged, stone steps. I was across the street; but, when I heard the voice of my child, I recognized her voice immediately. And I felt two powerful emotions. My first was a surge of adrenalin that made me jump to my feet and run to where she was screaming. But as I did so, there was also a flood of love in my heart because my little girl had cried out to me, her father. "Daddy!" was her immediate impulse.

I am certain that our Father in heaven, when he hears us cry out to him, feels the same emotions. Jehovah takes pleasure in our seeking him first. He is delighted when we run and take refuge in him. Our God loves us far more deeply than we can possibly know or conceive. And God's heart floods with love when we seek him and cry out for his deliverance. -- How horribly sad that most of the people we encounter everyday do not have what we do. Believers in Jesus are never alone. Our God, our Shepherd, our Maker, created mankind to be his family and to enjoy loving us all. God assures us that we are His by our receiving his Holy Spirit and a new birth. "**For he who sanctifies and those who are sanctified all have one source. That is why he is not ashamed to call them brothers.**" (Hebrews 2:11)

Jesus loves us and watches over us, as our father has asked him to do. "**Everyone the Father gives Me will come to Me, and the one who comes to Me I will never drive away. For I have come down from heaven, not to do My own will, but to do the will of Him who sent Me.**" (John 6:37) How wonderful to know this and to walk with him in peace and safety. This is the assurance we have received from Jesus: "**I am with you always!**" (Matthew 28:20) Jesus is always our *"hiding place"* and our *"shelter,"* and our *"refuge."*

Certainly, many of us have had close calls and encountered danger, even perhaps threats on our lives. Throughout the years, I have served thousands of US veterans who have had these experiences many times. I have had a few such experiences myself. Hurtful experiences from our past may have detrimental effects on us for decades. But because of Christ in our hearts, we can forgive and even forget, just as God does toward us. "**I, even I,** am he who blots out your transgressions, for my own sake, and remembers your sins no more." (Isaiah 43:25) We can forgive too, even when never asked to do so. Christ loves us far more than any mere human. His love will never fail. "**He satisfies my soul.**" (Psalm 107:9)

"O Lord my God, in You I have taken refuge; save me from all those who pursue me and deliver me." (verse 1) A better understanding of this verb tense in the original text indicates that David is saying with complete confidence that God has, and God will continue to be his "*refuge,*" and to "*deliver*" him from "*all those who pursue me.*" David is not calling out with doubt, but in faith. David's life was being threatened by King Saul with an army, and the most terrifying of his warriors, 'Cush.' David had witnessed and knew that no enemy could succeed in their threats against him with the Lord at his side.

David had known Jehovah since being a young boy. No doubt in his times as a shepherd, alone with sheep day after day and night after night, David spoke to God. He developed a total trust in God. That trust in Jehovah was the impetus and Muse for David as he wrote these songs.

When we are innocent, accused falsely, slandered, and sought after by those that want to do us harm, we must muster our faith. Prayer and singing hymns and worship songs help during these times. So, in the last verse of Psalm 7, David says, *"I will give thanks to the Lord according to His righteousness. And I will sing praise to the name of the Lord Most High."* (verse 8)

"We Have a Friend in Jesus" has been a favorite Christian hymn for 170 years. The third verse of the song seems to encapsulate the meaning of this Psalm: *"Are we weak and heavy-laden? Cumbered with a load of care? Precious Savior, still our refuge – Take it to the Lord in prayer; Do thy friends despise, forsake thee? Take it to the Lord in prayer. In His arms He'll take and shield thee, Thou wilt find a solace there."*

"Let the assembly of the peoples encompass You, and over them return on high." (verse 7) As a prophet, David knew about God's redemptive plan. He knew that one day God would reign on earth. Indeed, the Holy Spirit gave to David amazing revelations of Christ. David speaks of the need of mankind to bow in reverence before God's anointed Son. **"Kiss his son, or he will be angry, and your way will lead to your destruction, for his wrath can flare up in a moment. Blessed are all who take refuge in him."** (Psalm 2:12)

David also pleads his case before Jehovah by asking Him to **"Vindicate me, O Lord, according to my righteousness and my integrity that is in me."** (verse 8) In this Psalm and throughout the Bible we are told that 'God blesses the righteous.' He rewards them for repentance and their devotion to living in a way that pleases and glorifies the Lord. This is the **"*integrity*"** and **"*righteousness*"** for which David is pleading. Even though we are born into sin, if we earnestly yield to the work of the Holy Spirit inside of us, we become better people. We are honest in all our dealings. We walk in the ways of our Lord. Our ways of living and interacting with our loved ones, churches, and among the unbelieving are ripe with the fruit of God's righteousness within us. We hate to displease Jehovah, because we know that He is our life, our peace, and our joy. And we do this because: **"We know that the Son of God has come, and he has given us understanding so that we can know the true God. And now we live in fellowship with the true God because we live in fellowship with his Son, Jesus Christ. He is the only true God, and he is eternal life."** (John 5:20)

No one can make themselves righteous by force of human will, nor by religious practices and rituals. As the Apostle Peter says, our righteousness is the work of the Holy Spirit and that God has chosen us to be made into his image: **"You are all children of the light and children of the day. We do not belong to the night or to the darkness."** (1 Thessalonians 5:5) And the Apostle Peter says: **"But now you must be holy in everything you do, just as God who chose you is holy.**

For the Scriptures say, "You must be holy because I am holy." (1 Peter 1:5) Mankind has a choice: ***"My shield is with God, who saves the upright in heart. God is a righteous judge. And a God who has indignation every day. If a man does not repent, He will sharpen His sword; He has bent His bow and made it ready."*** (verses 10-12) Either we choose to repent and seek the one and only Creator and God, who became a man and revealed himself to us in the person of Jesus Christ, or we choose to deny this and live our lives according to our own will and refuse to believe in our Maker and Savior.

If we give our lives to Christ, He transforms us and sets us on a path righteousness: This is the straight and simple choice for everyone to make: ***"Those who belong to Christ Jesus have*** *nailed the passions and desires of their sinful nature to his cross and crucified them there.*" (Galatians 5:24) Or they can choose this: "*If a man does not repent, He will sharpen His sword; He has bent His bow and made it ready.*" (verse 12)

All of Jehovah's children should live harmless lives. We should always be seeking to live according to His will, and to be approved by Him. We must strive to be without blame and innocent. We are to respect all mankind, to pray for them, and to live lives that testify that we are indeed God's chosen children. "**Do not repay anyone evil for evil. Carefully consider what is right in the eyes of everybody. If it is possible on your part, live at peace with everyone. Do not avenge yourselves, beloved, but leave room for God's wrath. For it is written: "Vengeance is Mine; I will repay, says the Lord."** (Romans 12:18)

King David then closes this Psalm with. "*I will give thanks to the Lord according to His righteousness. And will sing praise to the name of the Lord Most High.*" (verse 17) This is the key to having a close, loving, intimate relationship with God. It is how we can overcome sin, sickness, broken hearts, pain, and assaults upon our integrity: Give thanks to Jehovah every day until you lay down to sleep. Praise Jehovah for His goodness to you. This is how we all become transformed into new creatures, no longer earthly, but heavenly citizens. – This is God's holy and immutable promise: "**Therefore, if anyone is in Christ, the new creation has come, the old has gone, and the new is here!**" (2 Corinthians 5:17)

Psalm 8

Wherever we look we can see the creative designs of the Great Artist of the universe, Jesus Christ. The translation of the word *"God"* in the Bible is what God answered Moses when he asked, "What is your name?" God's reply was *"I AM!"*: "I AM now, I have always Been, and I will always Be." (Exodus 3:14) Jesus uses this name for himself when he speaks to the seven churches in Revelation: **"I am the Alpha and the Omega – the beginning and the end,"** says the Lord God. **"I am the one who is, who always was, and who is still to come – the Almighty One."** (Revelation 1:8) Wherever we look, we can see the creative designs of this Great Artist of the universe, Jesus Christ.

In this Psalm, David expresses what most people have felt when alone and surrounded by Nature and the night sky: **"LORD, our Lord, how majestic is your name in all the earth!"** (verse 1) How can mortal words express the fullness and amazement of creation? What a *"majestic"* creator is our God!

When the Lord called Moses to bring the Jews back to their *"promised land."* The miracles he did in Egypt stunned the then known world! All the nations feared the God of Moses. And

Jehovah proved himself to the Jews in the wilderness for 40 years. He brought water from rocks, bread from heaven, quails; and their clothing, sandals and tents never wore out. He led them by fire at night and with his bright shining glory during the day.

After Moses died, Joshua led the Jewish people as they entered the Promised Land, with the children of those that entered the wilderness with Moses. Jehovah made a path through the Jordan river and brought down the walls of Jericho. The fear of the Jews and their mighty God terrified the known world!

These Jews who were once slaves to Pharaoh, had seen the blessings and the judgements of Jehovah. They had seen fire come from heaven and devour those that rebelled against Moses. And they had even seen the earth open and the rebels cast into Hell alive! They feared Jehovah too; so, should all who defy him.

One thing that generation knew: "**Hear, O' Israel, the Lord our God is One. There is no other!**" (Deuteronomy 6:4) And now, billions of *gentiles* (non-Jews), have believed too. We are the "**seed of Abraham**." (Romans 9:8) If we share Abraham's faith, then we are the chosen of God and his beloved children too. Our God is One. There is no other. Thus, our Lord and Savior Jesus Christ, God's begotten Son says, "**I and my Father are one**." (John 10:30) Our belief is that Jehovah is three in one (1=3). Father, Son, and Holy Spirit. And this oneness shared by the Holy Trinity is also the oneness that Christ desires for us. He prayed this for us: "…**that all of them may be one, as You, Father, are in Me, and I am in You. May they also be in Us, so that the world may believe that You sent Me. I have given them the glory You gave Me, so that they may one as we are one**." (John 17:21-22)

When David looked up at the night's brilliant firmament, he was speechless. "***LORD, our Lord, how majestic is your name in all the earth! You have set your glory in the heavens.***" (verse 1) The truth of God is written on all of our hearts. "**For when Gentiles who do not have the Law do instinctively the things of the Law, these, not having the Law, are a law to themselves, in that they show the work of the Law written in their hearts, their consciences bearing witness and their thoughts alternately accusing or else defending them, on the day when, according to my gospel, God will judge the secrets of men through Christ Jesus.**" (Romans 2:14-15)

Jehovah has these three distinct attributes, specific only to Himself: He is Omnipresent. Jehovah is everywhere in the entire Cosmos, in his personal fullness, all at the same time! That means that even if you were flown to Mars, and prayed to Jehovah, he would hear your prayers and answer. – How can Jehovah hear all the words lifted to him from across the world, listen to each one separately, and answer each one uniquely? He can because he is fully present everywhere!

Jehovah is Omniscient. He contains all the knowledge of everything. The Bible teaches us that: "***God hears our thoughts before we think them, knows our words before we speak them, and sees what we do before we do it. There is nothing we know that he does not. Nothing is hidden from Him.***" (Psalm 139) Jehovah knows all.

Jehovah is Omnipotent. He is the source of all power, energy, force, and life. Scientists and Astronomers have discovered so many universal laws that support existence; yet many will not concede the obvious truth behind them: God exists! An all knowing and all powerful being designed it all. Even the basis of their evolutionary theory, the "stuff" that mixed together to form the first cell: They have no answer from where it would have come from. "It just happened," is their extremely non-scientific answer. And when asked what "Black Matter" is, the invisible glue that holds the universe together and makes up 95% of the cosmos, their answer is, "We do not have any idea." – It is Jesus Christ. **"He is before all things, and in him all things hold together."** (Colossians 1:17)

David says, *"You have taught children and infants to tell of your strength, silencing your enemies and all who oppose you."* (verse 2) Children instinctively know God exists, especially when they look up towards the heavens at night. Even millions of grown adults, who have never heard the Gospel, know that there is a God when they look up and all around. They have a conscience too: The voice of God's Spirit telling them what is right and what is wrong. So, when these proud and extremely knowledgeable scientists stand before Jehovah one day and claim that they did not know or realize that there was a God, Jehovah will point to those children and untaught gentiles that did. *"How is it that these whom you considered fools knew, and you did not?"* The scientists will then be silent and suffer the judgement due to those who persist in denying our Creator's existence.

"What is mankind that you are mindful of them, human beings that you care for them? You have made them a little lower than the angels and crowned them with glory and

honor. You made them rulers over the works of your hands; you put everything under their feet." (verse 4-6) Mankind was created by our holy and divine Maker because he desires fellowship with beings made in His likeness. He made the Earth especially for us. On this unique and special planet, He created life. "Then God said, "**Let us make human beings in our own likeness, so that they may rule over the fish in the sea and the birds in the sky, over livestock and all wild animals, and over all creatures that move along the ground.**" (Genesis 1:26)

"*You have made them a little lower than the angels and crowned them with glory and honor.*" (verse 5) For now, angels are far more powerful than any human. They stand before the throne of God and receive their orders from Him. But when the fulfillment of time comes, and eternity is ushered in, then all believers in Christ will be changed into new creations and become mightier than angels. "**Do you not know that we are to judge angels? How much more then matters pertaining to this life.**" (1 Corinthians 6:3) Knowing this, David urges us to seriously consider how we live in this life; for, it determines our eternal future.

David then concludes this psalm in the same way as he began, "**LORD, our Lord, how majestic is your name in all the earth!**" (verse 9) The majesty of our God is contained in every facet of His character and behavior. But the core of God's majesty, as with our own, lies within His heart. "**God is love.**" (1 John 4:8)

Psalm 9

Regardless of what trials, afflictions, and difficulties we endure in life, God's redeemed have reason to rejoice and praise our God and Savior. This verse encapsulates the primary theme of this psalm. "**God will never forget the needy; the hope of the afflicted will never perish.**" (verse 18)

David is being hunted by Saul's army and his most ferocious warrior. Eventhough, he begins his Psalm with confidence: "*I will give thanks to you, LORD, with all my heart; I will tell of all your wonderful deeds. I will be glad and rejoice in you; I will sing the praises of your name, O Most High.*" (verses 1-2) David begins his plea as we always should when we come before the Lord, and as he does in almost all of his psalms, "**Enter into his gates with thanksgiving, and into his courts with praise: be thankful unto him, and bless his name.**" (Psalm 100:4) These are David's instructions on how to begin our prayers whenever we come before Jehovah, in all circumstances. We are encouraged to practice this throughout each day, so as to enable us to "**walk in the Spirit, rather than fulfill the lusts of our flesh.**" (Galatians 5:16)

In verse 3 and 4 David recalls the blessings he received from Jehovah when he had been threatened before: "***My enemies turn back; they stumble and perish before you. For you have upheld my right and my cause, sitting enthroned as the righteous judge.***" (verses 3-4) David comes before God with praise for what he has done for him. It is also a statement of confident faith. It is spoken emphatically, with this meaning: 'This is what God has done, is doing, and will continue to do for me again.'

It is our blessed comfort to know that God planned our life before the cosmos came into existence. There is nothing about us that Jehovah does not already know: "**Know that he is Lord, Jehovah our God, and it is he who has made us, and it was not we ourselves; we are his people and the sheep of his pasture.**" (Psalm 100:3) And "**For we are God's handiwork, created in Christ Jesus to do good works, which God prepared in advance for us to do.**" (Ephesians 2:10)

Christians know that the Maker of all that is seen, and unseen has chosen us to be

His. Christ has given us proof by the indwelling of His Holy Spirit. By His Spirit and His word, we know that he cares about us as a loving Father does; therefore, we are able to endure Life's hardships and tragedies. The events of our lives are not always seen as blessings. Certainly, the loss of loved ones never seems to be. Of course, it hurts terribly. Our God knows. Remember, "**Jesus wept**" at Lazarus' tomb. (John 11:35)

In all circumstances, regardless of how terrifying, difficult, or heartbreaking, we must continue to believe and walk in this assurance: "**And we know that all things work together for good to them that love God, to them who are called according to His purpose.**" (Romans 8:28) If we truly have faith in the word of Jehovah, then we must trust him, especially when things seem impossible to achieve or to endure.

Now, David foretells the reign of Christ, and gives us the same expectancy and hope that believers have had down through the Millenia: "*My enemies turn back; they stumble and perish before you. For you have upheld my right and my cause, sitting enthroned as the righteous judge. You have rebuked the nations and destroyed the wicked; you have blotted out their name for ever and ever. Endless ruin has overtaken my enemies, you have uprooted their cities; even the memory of them has perished. The LORD reigns forever; he has established his throne for judgment. He rules the world in righteousness and judges the peoples with equity. The LORD is a refuge for the oppressed, a stronghold in times of trouble.*" (verses 3-9) These verses ultimately speak of the return of the King of Kings to rule over the earth. David foresaw this glorious time of Jesus and his rule of righteousness and peace. This is called the "**Great Hope**" (Titus 2:13) of all believers, the coming reign of Jesus Christ on earth! – The Apostle John states: "**And everyone who has this hope fixed on Him purifies himself, just as He is pure.**" (1 John 3:3) It is the "**hope**" that gives us joy in the midst of sorrow and courage when we are afraid.

Although David is being hunted like a wild animal, he finds composure and confidence by bringing to mind the Lord's promises and prior proofs of this transcendent truth, "*The Lord is a refuge for the oppressed, a stronghold in times of trouble. Those who know your name trust in you, for you, Lord, have never forsaken those who seek you.*" (verse 10), David has considered Jehovah's prior and present blessings and thanked God for them. David has assured himself that Jehovah has always made his "*enemies turn back.*" (verse 3) He has made several statements of faith and comforted himself with the knowledge that the "*Lord abides forever*," (verse 7) And so will all those that trust in Jehovah. Jehovah is David's and our "*refuge* and *stronghold*;" (verse 9) and those that trust in Him "*have never been forsaken.*" (verse 10) --David reminds us of this and meditates on it as he faces the ordeal before him. It puts our lives in perspective. We too should always remind ourselves, whatever happens, that we will continue to be blessed forever! Just as David reminds himself, so should we in complete belief: "*Lord, you have not forsaken those who seek you.*" (verse 10)

As I write this, I preach three times a week to the poor, the old and lonely, the lame, and some veterans with serious PTSD, almost all of whom are struggling to support themselves and their families. Serving such as these is my "calling." It has been throughout my life. Many of these poor, humble people are the most sincere and devout Christians I have ever served. They fully understand David's need to strengthen himself by seeking the Lord and putting faith in God's promises. That faith is how they survive each day. Just as Christ and the early Christians were poor, rejected, and persecuted, so are they. They identify with the sufferings of Christ and the Apostles. By necessity, they grip the Lord's hand every day and put their total hope in Him to provide and to keep them alive.

Listen to the Apostle Paul describe the life that he and Christians lived during the tremendous outpouring of God's Spirit, as Paul and other Apostles established churches around the known world. "**In everything we do, we show that we are true ministers of God. We patiently endure troubles and hardships and calamities of every kind. We have been beaten, been put in prison, faced angry mobs, worked to exhaustion, endured sleepless nights, and gone without food. We prove ourselves by our purity, our understanding, our patience, our kindness, by the Holy Spirit within us, and by our sincere love. We faithfully preach the truth. God's power is working in us. We use the weapons of righteousness in the right hand for attack and the left hand for defense. We serve God whether people honor us or despise us, whether they slander us or praise us. We are honest, but they call us impostors. We are ignored, even though we are well known. We live close to death, but we are still alive. We have been beaten, but we have not been killed. Our hearts ache, but we always have joy. We are poor, but we give spiritual riches to others. We own nothing, and yet we have everything.**" (2 Corinthians 6:4-10) Some are blessed with riches. Some are blessed with poverty.

When God took everything Job had, this is how he responded: "**Naked I came from my mother's womb, and naked I shall return there. The LORD gave, and the LORD has taken away. Blessed be the name of the LORD." Through all this Job did not sin nor did he blame God.**" (Job 1:21)

There is a saying in the military, "When the going gets tough, the tough get going." In these last days, a sword will come upon the Christian Church, worldwide. There will be a separation between his "Sheep" the truly chosen of God, and the "Goats, who have deceived themselves into thinking that are too." Please look carefully within your heart as you read this parable Jesus gave: **"But when the Son of Man comes in his glory, and all the holy angels with him, then he will sit on the throne of his glory. Before him, all the nations will be gathered, and he will separate them one from another, as a shepherd separates the sheep from the goats. He will set the sheep on his right hand, but the goats on the left. Then the King will tell those on his right hand, 'Come, blessed of my Father, inherit the Kingdom prepared for you from the foundation of the world; for I was hungry, and you gave me food to eat. I was thirsty, and you gave me drink. I was a stranger, and you took me in. I was naked, and you clothed me. I was sick, and you visited me. I was in prison, and you came to me.' Then the righteous will answer him, saying, 'Lord, when did we see you hungry, and feed you; or thirsty, and give you a drink? When did we see you as a stranger, and take you in; or naked, and clothe you? When did we see you sick, or in prison, and come to you?' "The King will answer them, 'Most certainly I tell you, because you did it to one of the least of these my brothers, you did it to me.' Then he will say also to those on the left hand, 'Depart from me, you cursed, into the eternal fire which is prepared for the devil and his angels; for I was hungry, and you didn't give me food to eat; I was thirsty, and you gave me no drink;**

I was a stranger, and you didn't take me in; naked, and you didn't clothe me; sick, and in prison, and you didn't visit me.' "Then they will also answer, saying, 'Lord, when did we see you hungry, or thirsty, or a stranger, or naked, or sick, or in prison, and didn't help you?' "Then he will answer them, saying, 'Most certainly I tell you, because you didn't do it to one of the least of these, you didn't do it to me.' These will go away into eternal punishment, but the righteous into eternal life."** (Matthew 25:31-46)

It is an embarrassment and a shame when churches ignore the needs of the poor within their own churches. What they do not seem to understand is that those who are poor and rejected may be the cornerstone of their church. They share in the suffering and rejection of Christ. They by necessity, seek the Lord constantly. So, to the Church which practices "brotherly love," (the Church at Philadelphia), Jesus promises: **"I have opened a door no one can close. I will force those of the Synagogue of Satan to bow down at your feet and acknowledge you are the ones I love. I will protect you from the great time of testing that will come upon the whole world."** (Revelation 3:10)

This is what poor, afflicted, and persecuted Christians are told by the Holy Spirit in Psalm 9: *"**For He who avenges blood remembers them. He does not forget the cry of the afflicted and abused.**"* (verse 9) And again, *"**For the poor will not always be forgotten, nor the hope of the burdened perish forever.**"* (verse 18)

David closes with a prayer for the unsaved: "***The wicked will turn to Sheol*** (the nether world, the place of the dead), ***even*** *all the nations who forget God.... Put them in fear of You, O Lord, so that the nations may know they are but frail and mortal men."* (verses 17-20) David, asks for them what we must also ask every day for the unsaved.

Fellow Christian brothers and sisters always remember that we are not to be 'natural people' like everyone else. We are blessed to have the Holy Spirit of God within; therefore, we are to be 'super-natural' people. Jesus says, **"You have heard that it was said, 'Love your neighbor and hate your enemy.' But I tell you, love your enemies and pray for those who persecute you, that you may be children of your Father in heaven. He causes his sun to rise on the evil and the good and sends rain on the righteous and the unrighteous. If you love those who love you, what reward will you get? Are not even the tax collectors doing that? And if you greet only your own people, what are you doing more than others? Do not even pagans do that? Be perfect even as your Father in Heaven is perfect."** (Matthew 5:43-48)

Psalm 10

It has always been difficult for many people to understand why bad things happen to good people. "How is that just and fair? How can God permit this?" David asks a similar question here, "*Why, Lord, do you stand far off? Why do you hide yourself in times of trouble? In his pride and arrogance, the wicked man hunts down and persecutes the weak and the poor, who are caught in the schemes he devises.*" (verses 1-2) This Psalm concerns itself with the wicked wealthy, who crush the helpless. David is deeply concerned about those in his land who suffered from poverty, just as is the Lord Himself. God commanded Moses to declare this statute, "**If among you, one of your brothers should become poor, in any of your towns within your land that the Lord your God is giving you, you shall not harden your heart or shut your hand against your poor brother, but you shall open your hand to him and lend him sufficient for his need, whatever it may be ... For the poor you will always have with you in the land. Therefore, I command you, 'You shall open wide your hand to your brother, to the needy and to the poor, in your land.**" (Deuteronomy 15:7-11) "*He boasts about the cravings of his heart; he blesses the greedy and reviles the Lord. In his pride the* *wicked man does not seek him; in all his thoughts there is no room for God."* (verses 3-4) The bite of riches frequently poisons the hearts and minds of those who have the means to live much better lifestyles than their less fortunate neighbors. They even have slogans like: *"The one who has the most toys when he dies wins!"* Their source of confidence and pride is determined by the value of the worldly possession they have hoarded. That is what makes them think that the poor are inferior humans who do not deserve their kindness and concern. This Psalm enumerates the evils and the proud attitudes of the people who own a treasure of worldly goods, but do not care for the poor. They will not endure forever. *"The Lord is King for ever and ever; the nations will perish from his land. You, Lord, hear the desire of the afflicted; you encourage them, and you listen to their cry; defending the fatherless and the oppressed, so that mere earthly mortals will never again strike terror."* (verses 16-18)

The rich have the resources that protect them from seeing the true nature of their lives. Many are proud, rather than humble. They do not know that in the eyes of the Lord they are not first, but last. As Jesus states in Matthew 20:16 "**So those who are last now will be first then, and those who are first now will be last.**" However, this Psalm is meant to encourage the poor, more than as it is to accuse the rich. For what many wealthy people do not understand is that being poor in the world's riches can make one rich in eternal things. The real purpose of this psalm is in its conclusion: *"You, Lord, hear the desire of the afflicted; you encourage them, and you listen to their cry, defending the fatherless and the oppressed."* (verses

17-18) Many of us are poor in earthly riches; but, stored up in heaven is our reward, and our treasure. The Lord will lift us up. We now have the assurance and confidence to preach to the poor and say, "The Lord sees and knows everything about our life. He has not forsaken you. Put your trust in him. He is your strength. He is your hope. He will reward you for your patient endurance. Do not fear or despise your condition in life. Praise the Lord for what you do have. You are being blessed like the Apostles if you walk in faith." -- (This verse strengthens me when I am afraid, "**Wait, for the Lord. Yes, be strong and courageous. Wait for the Lord.**" Psalm 27:14)

When we suffer do not think God no longer loves us. Consider it a blessing to be treated like Christ. As Peter writes: "**Rejoice in as much as you participate in the sufferings of Christ, so that you may be overjoyed when his glory is revealed.**" (1 Peter 4:13) Remember how our Lord, who had no sin, was treated too. Rejoice when we get to share that experience with our Savior. Do not get off the straight and narrow. Remember this passage, "**Keep your life free from the love of money, and be content with what you have, for he has said, "I will never leave you nor forsake you.**" (Hebrews 13:5)

This is how Jesus as a man is described in Isaiah, "**He grew up before him like a tender shoot, and like a root out of dry ground. He had no beauty or majesty to attract us to him, nothing in his appearance that we should desire him. He was despised and rejected by mankind, a man of sorrows, and acquainted with grief. Like one from whom people hide their faces he was despised, and we held him in low esteem.**

Surely, he took up our pain and bore our suffering, yet we considered him punished by God, stricken by him, and afflicted. But he was pierced for our transgressions, he was crushed for our iniquities; the punishment that brought us peace was on him, and by his wounds we are healed." (Isaiah 53:1-5) If you are Christian who is hated, despised, and treated badly by others, even by other "Christians, be encouraged and rejoice. This is a blessing because you are sharing in the sorrows and rejection of our God and Savior, Jesus Christ. That is how the religious, and the leaders of the people of his day also treated Him.

Jesus was a "**man of sorrows and acquainted with grief.**" (Isaiah 53:3) He was often homeless and slept on the ground beneath the night sky. Yet, he was our Creator and the Savior of all mankind. He was the only perfectly righteous human that ever lived. In the Gospel of John, Jesus says, "**That is why the world hates you. Remember what I told you: 'A servant is not greater than his master. 'If they persecuted me, they will persecute you also.**" (John 15:19-20)

Christians who endure hardships, trials, tribulation, rejection, and pain will be rewarded when the Lord returns. In the Resurrection, our bodies will shine in power and glory. "***You, God, see the trouble of the afflicted; you consider their grief and take it in hand…You, Lord, hear the desire of the afflicted; you encourage them, and you listen to their cry.***" (verses 14 & 17)

Psalm 11

The Psalms are unique in that they give us an intimate insight into the heart of a man that pursued the Lord and righteousness. In many ways Christians throughout history have been comforted and strengthened by them. In these psalms, we read about a life that went through a myriad of trials, the life of a man with whom we can all relate. A man who persevered, despite his fears, assaults, and how many times he failed. David always got back up again to follow the ways of the Lord.

I am comforted and strengthened by reading the Psalms. David had doubts, fears, questions, struggles, sins, and suffered the chastisement of the Lord. But he possessed a faith given to him by God. A faith he nurtured until the end. Do we also have a faith with which we also grip unto the hand of the Lord? This psalm will help us know how to do so.

Psalm 11 relates to when David was in the court of King Saul. Saul was tormented by a demon and had frightening fits of rage, which he often directed at David, of whom he was envious and jealous. Apparently, some of those near David were encouraging him to flee from Saul's palace. Some pleaded with David because they loved him and were concerned. Others did so to bring disgrace to him, hoping that if David fled, either Saul would pursue him and kill him; or it would bring accusations against David that he was a coward and a traitor. Fortunately, David did not listen to either side. Instead, he answered them by writing this Psalm, in which he declares his confidence in God's overseeing Providence.

"In the Lord I take refuge. How then can you ask me to "Flee like a bird to your mountain." (verse 1) This is David's forceful retort to those who urged him to do so, ***"For look, the wicked bend their bows; they set their arrows against the strings to shoot from the shadows at the upright in heart."*** (verse 2) David was filled with purpose. He is to be the leader and an example to his people of a righteous ruler. And he was to shepherd them as he did his sheep when he was a boy. David was willing to lay down his life for them. He would not ***"Flee as a bird."***

David was acutely aware that he had enemies, especially Saul. This is the conflict faced by David and ourselves too: the upright vs. the wicked. During David's time, Israel was not being led by a righteous king. Saul abandoned the Lord. He consulted with witches for wisdom, instead of the Lord. Saul was tormented by demons. Therefore, David says, ***"When the foundations are being destroyed, what can the righteous do?"*** (verse 3) The foundations he speaks of are the laws of the Lord: the laws of righteousness and equal justice for all. – This is why David did not flee. Who would there be to speak the truth, and eventually rule with justice if he did? David persevered at King Saul's court because of his commitment to God and to His people.

Of this David was absolutely certain: *"The Lord is in his holy temple; the Lord is on his heavenly throne. He observes everyone on earth; his eyes examine them."* (verse 4) He knew that God is ultimately in charge. Nothing is hidden from Him, even the most secret of our thoughts are plainly heard by God. David trusted in God's plan and purpose for his life. Wicked men surrounded him on all sides. But who should David be concerned about: men or God?

"The Lord examines the righteous, but the wicked, those who love violence, he hates with a passion. On the wicked he will rain fiery coals and burning sulfur; a scorching wind will be their lot." (verses: 5-6) There is a day when the Lord's patience with unbelievers and the evil they practice will come to an end. That day is rapidly approaching. – People may argue with me about how soon that day will come. But the Lord continually warns us to be ready. **"Therefore, be on the alert, for you do not know which day your Lord is coming. But be sure of this, that if the head of the house had known at what time of the night the thief was coming, he would have been on the alert and would not have allowed his house to be broken into. For this reason, you also must be ready; for the Son of Man is coming at an hour when you do not think He will. "Who then is the faithful and sensible slave whom his master put in charge of his household to give them their food at the proper time? Blessed is that slave whom his master finds so doing when he comes. Truly I say to you that he will put him in charge of all his possessions. But if that evil slave says in his heart, 'My master is not coming for a long time,' and begins to beat his fellow slaves and eat and drink**

with drunkards; the master of that slave will come on a day when he does not expect him and at an hour which he does not know, and will cut him in pieces and assign him a place with the hypocrites; in that place there will be weeping and gnashing of teeth." (Matthew 24: 42-51)

I am aware of how the unbelieving mock our belief. Even when I was a child such Christians were ridiculed. I recall reading the cartoons and frequently seeing a joke about a man on a street corner holding a sign that said something like, "Repent! The End is coming!" Most people saw this cartoon and laughed out loud. But they are much more likely to take it seriously today. The world's "climatologists" adamantly insist that the earth is not just experiencing a change in the weather. Rather, they say, "Global warming' is an extinction event!" And now we have seen the Corona Virus take hundreds of thousands of lives across the world. Every prediction in the Bible about the end of this earth and mankind's reign upon it will be fulfilled in our time. Christians await a new earth and the reign of Jesus Christ on earth, a kingdom that will last forever.

I believe that the generation that saw the reestablishment of Israel as a nation shall not die off before Jesus Christ returns to reign. The bible promises that those who witness Israel become a nation again and blossom like a garden, **"this generation will not pass away until all these things have happened. Heaven and earth will pass away, but My words will never pass away."** (Matthew 24:33-35) God has a plan in place.

David closes this Psalm with a statement of conviction and faith: *"For the Lord is righteous, he loves justice; the upright will see his face."* Our God, Jehovah, is righteous. He is absolutely perfect in all that He does. How can we ever doubt that when we see the micro and macro cosmos? Everything fits together and runs in perfect harmony. The cosmos is not the result of "random chance and chaos," as the unbelieving insist. It is proof of the glorious majesty and power of the Lord! **"All the paths of the Lord are steadfast love and faithfulness."** (Psalm 25:10)

God is a holy. He cares about the poor, the rejected, dismissed, persecuted, afflicted, and immigrants. These are the "lower class." That is why Jesus associated with such. He loves them. He touched and healed lepers. He had compassion on the lame, the sick, the blind, immigrants, and the aged. These are the ones that often do not receive equal justice. These are those our Savior especially loves.

Our nation's court systems often makes criminals out of the poor and innocent. The homeless are always persecuted and treated worse than most other members of our society. When they are arrested, the D.A. sends one of their attorneys down to the holding cells at the court before they see the judge. (This is how D.A.s improve their conviction record.) They go to those that they know do not have attorneys: those that are too poor to do so. Then they say something like this: "If you plead guilty right now, I will let you go home today. If you do not, you may have to remain in jail for months before your case can be tried. What do you want to do?" Of course, most poor people who cannot afford an attorney will take this offer, regardless if they are guilty or innocent. -- Is this the "justice" that the Lord desires? No.

Before I close, let me put some balance to what I have taught here. Being wealthy is the calling and purpose of some Christians. Their riches are to be used to bless others, not just themselves. Certainly, not all rich people are evil. Instead, they have been blessed so they can bless others. But it is a test for them. Just as being poor is also a test of our faith. Jesus said that we "will always have the poor," until he returns. For some of us that is where God wants us to be.

Whether we are rich, poor, or in between, our calling is to thank the Lord and to praise His name. This verse and warning from Malachi is for all of us. We are to live in honesty, compassion, and integrity, regardless of our situation, without excuse. **"So, I will come to put you on trial. I will be quick to testify against… those who defraud laborers of their wages, who oppress the widows and the fatherless, and deprive the foreigners among you of justice, but do not fear me," says the Lord Almighty."** (Malachi 3:5)

The Apostle Paul writes: **"Remember, dear brothers and sisters, that few of you were wise in the world's eyes or powerful or wealthy when God called you. Instead, God chose things the world considers foolish in order to shame those who think they are wise. And he chose things that are powerless to shame those who are powerful. God chose things despised by the world, things counted as nothing at all, and used them to bring to nothing what the world considers important. As a result, no one can ever boast in the presence of God."** (1 Corinthians 1:26-29) This is a critical verse for Christian believers. Paul is clearly stating that few Christians will be "powerful or wealthy." Whereas most Christians will be powerless, poor, and considered "fools" by worldly unbelievers. -- Praise the Lord! Love and pray for all and a great reward will be waiting for us in heaven if we do.

I associate with some financially successful Christians. They are humble servants of the Lord. They experience the concern and love that God has put into their hearts to turn and to lift up the less fortunate. We are working together to build businesses for US veterans. We assist US veterans in starting successful businesses because we want them to employ as many hardworking veterans as they can. Most veterans have respect for each other and are more likely to pay veterans better wages. This is noble. This honors the Lord. – I am fortunate that a few "rich" Christians have been called to help me to help others too. We share the same heart and "calling."

"*The Lord examines the righteous, but the wicked, those who love violence, he hates with a passion.*" (verse 5) Whether we are rich or poor, young, or old, popular, or despised, free, or oppressed, the most paramount thing is to love all others with the love of Jesus Christ. We are to be humble and know that we have all been called by God to be used for His purposes and glory. If we turn away, then we only have a terrible future ahead for eternity. "*No one who puts a hand to the plow and looks back is fit for service in the kingdom of God.*" (Luke 9:62)

"*For the Lord is righteous, he loves justice; the upright will see his face.*" (verse 7) The "*upright*" do what Jesus would do. They practice righteousness in their personal lives and defend those that are persecuted unjustly. The "*upright*" defend the poor, the widow, the orphan, the homeless, and the persecuted. Do we? Or do we judge them to be less worthy than ourselves? Remember what the apostle James says, **"Pure religion and undefiled before God and the Father is this, to visit the fatherless and widows in their affliction, and to keep himself unspotted from the world."** (James 1:27)

Psalm 12

"**Help, Lord**" (verse 1) How precious are those that seek our Maker, who practice self-control over what they say and do, so that they please the Lord. When we cry out to God, be certain that He hears us. Our hardships, fears and troubles are the concern of Jehovah. He is our shield and our protector. David complains about the ungodly behavior of many in his kingdom. *"For no one is faithful anymore; those who are loyal have vanished from the human race. Everyone lies to their neighbor; they flatter with their lips but harbor deception in their hearts. May the LORD silence all flattering lips and every boastful tongue—those who say, "By our tongues we will prevail; our own lips will defend us—who is lord over us?"* (verse 2-4) Israel and Judah served the Lord in righteousness for only a short time before they turned away. Most of the Bible is an exhortation to repent and to return to serving our Maker, the One who is the source of all life. As the chosen of Christ, and as His witnesses to all the world, we must seek holiness earnestly. A vessel with cracks and leaks cannot be used to carry water; and so, we who carry the good news of God must be trustworthy in all that we say; for, we carry the "Living Water." "**Anyone who is thirsty** may come to me! Anyone who believes in me may come and drink! For the Scriptures declare, 'Rivers of living water will flow from his heart." (John 7:37-38)

David claims that many of these flattering deceivers take advantage of the poor. **"Because the poor are plundered and the needy groan, I will now arise," says the Lord. "I will protect them from those who malign them."** (verse 5) David assures the persecuted that they can trust God's promises. ***And the words of the Lord are flawless, like silver purified in a crucible, like gold refined seven times.*** (verse 6)

We must choose between believing and trusting our Creator or not. As Moses said to the people who left Egypt and crossed the Red Sea, **"This day I call the heavens and the earth as witnesses against you that I have set before you life and death, blessings and curses. Now choose life, so that you and your children may live and that you may love the Lord your God, listen to his voice, and hold fast to him; for the LORD is your life."** (Deuteronomy 30:19-20) The practice of deception is rampant on the earth. It always has been. More than 2000 years ago, the Roman poet, Virgil, made a similar statement: "*Justice has fled, and the truth is no more.*" -- Today, we have the technology to broadcast across the globe with a touch of a button. Falsehood and lies are now more prevalent than ever before. We are saturated with deception. We are at war against "fake news." It is almost impossible to determine what is real and what is not.

"They speak vanity everyone with his neighbor: with flattering lips and with a double heart do they speak." (verse 2) Simply understood: 'They say one thing; but their secret purpose is entirely something else.' It is the defect of character that the "son of the morning" (Satan) had, and what caused him to be cast from heaven to his ultimate doom. What we say and how we say it comes from our hearts. Jesus taught us, **"A good man out of the good treasure of his heart brings forth good; and an evil man out of the evil treasure of his heart brings forth evil. For out of the abundance of the heart his mouth speaks."** (Luke 6:45)

What we say shines forth what we believe, and who we really are. If we have died to selfishness and been born again to live for and to love God, then we have wrestled with what comes out of our mouths. Our words can be comforting and wholesome, or they can be like a razor-sharp sword that slashes and wounds. **"Those who consider themselves religious and yet do not keep a tight rein on their tongues deceive themselves, and their religion is worthless."** (James 1:26) In Psalm 12 **"*Flattering lips,*"** (verse 2) means "*words spoken without sincerity, integrity, and conviction.*" It is what we say to others for selfish and secret purposes. "***With a double heart do they speak.***" (verse 2 NASB) – Some of us must be in business with those that spurn the Lord. They are mockers of His word. They think of us as "fools" because we pray and urge them to "trust in God." But they do not say what they really think of us aloud. Instead, we are heaped with compliments and praise. They *flatter* us for hidden purposes with the intent to take what is not theirs. Try to see into their hearts of those you trust. Our first instinct is to **"be ready to believe the best in every person."** (1 Corinthians 13:7) Consequently, we are vulnerable to being used for deceptive purposes. Too frequently, those flatters succeed. All that we possess has been given to us by Jehovah; hence, when they lie and steal from us, they are actually doing so to their Maker and Judge. Let us leave them in his hands, and not take revenge ourselves. If we believe what they have taken was a gift from God, then He will restore to us again what they have taken. We can do this because Jesus provides us enough confidence and trust in Him to **"Do not resist evil. Whosoever shall smite thee on thy right. cheek, turn to him the other also."** (Matthew 5:39)

Flattery is lying. If we say something positive about someone, let it be true. If we earn someone's trust, do not take advantage and use it to take what is not ours. Beware! It is easy to deceive ourselves about our true intentions. Believers are wise to heed what Jesus taught: **" Beware of false prophets** (those that speak falsely). **They come to you in sheep's clothing, but inwardly they are ravenous wolves. By their fruit you will recognize them. Are grapes gathered from thorn bushes, or figs from thistles?"** (Matthew 7: 15-16) Those that practice lying will not enter the Kingdom of God.

Those who seek after the Lord are precious to God. He watches over them. **"His plans for us are to help us, not to hurt us."** (Jeremiah 29:11) Indeed, we of all people are the 'most blessed and fortunate.' Therefore, we do not seek after the things of this sinful and dying world. We desire one thing above all else: **"You shall love the Lord your God with all your heart, with all your soul, and with all your strength."** (Deuteronomy 6:5) Those who do so shall receive this promise, *"**You, LORD, will keep the needy safe and will protect us forever from the wicked, who freely strut about when what is vile is honored by the human race.**"* (verses 7-8)

Psalm 13

Here we are again, David lifts up a familiar lament, just as we do too. This is a common plea that God always hears from those who seek Him. *"**How long, Lord?**"* (verse 1) It is our breaking point. In the military and in athletics we know that in order to win it takes an immense amount of sacrifice and pain. We are continually encountering breaking points. That is what we reach for. "There is no gain without pain." For every human on earth this is true. It is how lasting growth happens. -- Why should it be any different when we seek to be strong in the Lord and to develop our faith? *"**How long, LORD? Will you forget me forever? How long will you hide your face from me?**"* (verse 1) This is David's breaking point. The Lord has not "forgotten" David. Nor is the Lord "hiding his face" from David. *"**How long will my enemy triumph over me; saying, "I have overcome him;" and rejoice when I fall?**"* (verse 4) The *"**enemy**"* that afflicts us is sin: the sin in others and the sins in ourselves. Whatever "enemy" we encounter, it comes from the same source: Sin. Therefore, we must not limit the meaning of any Psalm as only applicable to just David in his particular circumstance. It applies to every reader and to every fearsome hardship, trial, and test through which we must pass.

"But I trust in your unfailing love; my heart rejoices in your salvation. I will sing the LORD's praise, for he has been good to me." (verses 5-6) Suddenly, the entire tone and attitude of this Psalm changes. Something profound has happened between the first four verses of David's complaint and plea, and the "love, "salvation," and "good" for which David praises the Lord in the last two verses of Psalm 13. I suspect that David paused and was quiet before the Lord between verses 1-4 and 5-6. In Psalm 46 David quotes what the Lord says to him in the midst of his anxiety and unease. *"Be still and know that I am God."* (Psalm 46:10)

Our God is full of loving kindness towards us. He always hears whenever we cry out, *"How long must I wrestle with my thoughts and day after day have sorrow in my heart? How long will my enemy triumph over me?"* (verse 2) Our Father in heaven will be patient as we pour out our sorrow, confusion, and fear. It is important that we do so when we cannot hold it within us any longer. But then we must allow for the Holy Spirit to compose our hearts and souls. The Lord will answer us; but we must be still for a while and remember one thing: Know that the eternal I AM (Jehovah) is our God. Let us turn our eyes away from our troubles and worries and consider our God in these times. "And the things of earth will grow strangely dim, in the light of His glory and grace." ("Turn Your Eyes upon Jesus": Helen Lemmel)

Psalm 14

"*The fool says in his heart, "There is no God."* (verse 1) Before we begin seeking to understand this Psalm, in order to gain spiritual knowledge, let us read Psalm 14 with compassion for "*the fool.*" Were we not also fools once? All sin, in believers and unbelievers, begins with our listening to a voice that says, "There is no God who sees or hears." Christians also are "fools" sometimes. Every person has wondered if there is really a God who cares, a God who loves us with a greatness that we cannot comprehend. Even David encountered times in his life when he also felt like the God in heaven was not on his side. Fortunately, Christians do not live by what their minds think, and their hearts feel. We stand on the solid Rock of God's word. We put our trust in what God knows and how He feels. The Bible is His living word to us. It is our daily food and water that nourishes our souls. -- Before we believed, remember that this was true for us also: "***All have turned away, all have become corrupt; there is no one who does good, not even one.***" (verse 3) We were saved by God's grace and nothing else. It was not of our own will; but it was by the will of God. So, let us not stand in judgement of sinners. Instead, let us approach them as did our Savior who testified:

"For God did not send his Son into the world to condemn the world, but to save the world through him." (John 3:17)

There is a definite distinction between the foolish "***evildoers***" and the "***the poor***" whose refuge is the Lord. "***Do all these evildoers know nothing? They devour my people as though eating bread; they never call on the Lord. But there they are, overwhelmed with dread, for God is present in the company of the righteous. You evildoers frustrate the plans of the poor, but the Lord is their refuge.***" (verse 4-6) Certainly, the majority of humanity seeks after the gods (idols) of this world who can give them comfort and pleasure, instead of seeking the one and only God, who is righteous, good, and full of love. In fools' vain pursuit of these things they '***devour***" others. Whereas God's people are the "***righteous***" who take "***refuge***" in Lord. The "***dread***" by which "***evil doers will be "overwhelmed***" (verse 5) is the judgement they will encounter when they see "***the company of the righteous***" in the presence of God on the day that all mankind will be judged by the deeds that they did. Those that have plundered and frustrated the humble, the afflicted, the alien, the outcast, and the poor, will experience a terrible fear and "***dread.***"

It is true that before we are regenerated by receiving the Spirit of Christ into our hearts and lives, we too had no fear of God. The man of the world rejects the consciousness of what pleases and displeases his Maker. Those who practice evil refuse to even consider God. As Jesus says, **"For everyone who does evil hates the Light, and does not come to the Light for fear that his deeds will be exposed."** (John 3:20) Such people are the enemies of God. Their destiny is eternal darkness. These are the ones to whom we are to testify about the grace of God received through faith in his Son, Jesus Christ. **"For if while we were enemies we were reconciled to God through the death of His Son, much more, having been reconciled, we shall be saved by His life."** (Romans 5:10) Let us never think of ourselves as better than any other. We are not called to be masters. Christians are called to be humble servants. We too are sinners, in vital need of God to save us. **"You, therefore, have no excuse, you who pass judgment on someone else; for, at whatever point you judge another, you are condemning yourself because you who pass judgment do the same things."** (Romans 2:1) We who have received this greatest gift of all should be filled with excitement and an enthusiasm to share our Good News with everyone who does not know or understand. The grace that we have discovered through the redemption found in God's Son we should share with everyone that will listen.

The primary thing our Lord and Master has asked us to do is to **"Go and make disciples of all nations, baptizing them in the name of the Father and of the Son and of the Holy Spirit, and teaching them to obey everything I have commanded you."** (Matthew 28:19-20) First, we **"make disciples."** This is accomplished by preaching the Gospel, the Good News of Jehovah's gift of salvation and eternal life through the death and resurrection of His Son, the Creator. Then we are to **"baptize"** those that believe, so that they can receive the Holy Spirit and become born again. For only when we have the guidance and strength of God's Spirit can we please God and **"obey everything I have commanded you."**

The only way for anyone to cross over from seeking the temporary pleasures of this world, to be regenerated by God's eternal Spirit, and to be looking with hope and eager expectation for the coming reign of the "*Righteous One,*" is to believe this: **"God loves the people of this world so much that he sent his only and beloved Son to become a human and to provide a Way for us to be reunited with him forever."** (John 3:16 Living Bible) The Holy One of Heaven became one of us. He permitted we "fools" to crucify Him. This was His purpose: To pay a penalty that no one can afford: **"For the wages of sin is death, but the gift of God is eternal life in Christ Jesus our Lord."** (Romans 6:23) There is no other religion, philosophy, or way. Jesus said it simply and plainly: "**I am the way, the truth, and the life: no one can come to the Father apart from believing in me.**" (John 14:6)

The Apostle Paul came to Greece to win their hearts and minds for Christ. The apostle "**was resolved to know nothing while I was with you except Jesus Christ and him crucified.**" (1 Corinthians 2:2) Paul began his ministry in Greece by teaching the Love of God revealed in the sacrifice of Christ on the cross. He also begins his letter to the Romans in much the same way: "**Don't you see how wonderfully kind, tolerant, and patient God is with you? Does this mean nothing to you? Can't you see that God's kindness** (love) **is intended to turn you from your sin?**" (Romans 2:4)

We cannot turn anyone from sin by guilt. Almost everyone has the consciousness of there being a living, righteous God who will reward or condemn us when we die, even in the heart of those who declare that "***There is no God.***" (verse 1) When we confirm their guilt by beginning with God's condemnation and judgement, we turn more people away than we attract. Any believer whose faith is based on fear cannot walk in God's Spirit. That person will constantly fail at becoming *"a new creation in Christ Jesus."* (2 Corinthians 5:17) Instead, let us begin with the love of God. Help the unbelieving to see the many mercies of God surrounding them, and the wonderful and eternal life He has planned for their future.

The secret to effectively sharing of God's Good News with unbelievers (and believers too) is to be where they are, and to identify with what they think and feel. Were we not once like them? Have we not also wrestled with our sins? So, let us share the free gift of God with compassion, and not with judgement. **"Therefore, brothers and sisters, we have an obligation— but it is not to the flesh, to live according to it. For if you live according to the flesh, you will die; but if by the Spirit you put to death the misdeeds of the body, you will live. For those who are led by the Spirit of God are the children of God. The Spirit you received does not make you slaves, so that you live in fear again; rather, the Spirit you received brought about your adoption to sonship. And by him we cry, "Abba Father (Daddy)." The Spirit himself testifies with our spirit that we are God's children."** (Romans 8:12-17)

"Oh, that salvation for Israel would come out of Zion!" (verse 7a) David prays for the end of evil by the coming reign of heaven's Holy King. Jesus, the Creator of all that is seen and unseen. Heaven's Holy One will return and restore our

earth to a beauty it has never had. This is the "Blessed Hope" of all believers in Jehovah. **"We wait for the blessed hope--the appearing of the glory of our great God and Savior, Jesus Christ**." (Titus 2:13) All the instruments of war will be burned. No one will teach war anymore. It will be a wonderful world of peace. God's word even says that the animals will eat grass, instead of meat. Children can play with lions, bears, even snakes, and they will not be harmed. But before this great goodness comes down from above, God's patience with evil and those that practice sin will end. The Bible claims that the last seven years of this earth will be a final testing for humanity. People will have to choose between eternal life, by believing and trusting in Christ; or, to continue to rebel and suffer eternal torment and death. Satan is about to make his last stand against Jehovah's rule. Here is how Jesus describes it: "**For then there will be a great tribulation, such as has not occurred since the beginning ... for it will be a time of great suffering, such as has not occurred since men were upon the earth.**" (Matthew 24:21) However, in the Revelation of the Apostle John, Jesus promises his followers, "**Since you have kept my command to endure patiently, I will also keep you from the hour of trial that is going to come on the whole world to test the inhabitants of the earth.**" (Revelation 3:10) -Praise God! The children of God will be spared from this terrible time when God's wrath is poured out upon the evildoers of the earth. After that time, Christ and those who love Him will descend from heaven and enjoy His reign of peace and righteousness on earth. We will be given immortal bodies. Death will be no more. All suffering and sorrow will pass away. Therefore, David reminds and encourages us in the last line of his psalm: "***When the Lord restores his people, let Jacob rejoice and Israel be glad!***" (verse 7b) -- All believers in Christ are also "***Israel.***" Every blessing in the bible belongs to those who belong to Christ. For this, let us with Israel always "***be glad!***"

Psalm 15

"*Lord, who may dwell in your sacred tent? Who may live on your holy mountain?*" (verse 1) This is a small psalm. It plainly states how a Godly person behaves. It especially focuses on how we use our tongue, also a small thing. The Bible teaches us that what we speak reveals what is in our heart. If we speak badly about others, especially of fellow saints, we commit a serious sin. In truth, perhaps the easiest sin to commit is with our tongue. "**No human being can tame the tongue. It is a restless evil, full of deadly poison.**" (James 5:8)

"*The one whose walk is blameless, who does what is righteous, who speaks the truth from their heart, whose tongue utters no slander, who does no wrong to a neighbor, and casts no slur on others.* (verses 2-3) In truth, no one can do "*what is righteous*" and refrain from sin without first being clothed in the righteousness of Christ and receiving his Holy Spirit. By the will of our fleshly minds and bodies we will never "*walk with integrity, and work righteousness, and speak truth in our heart.*" (verse 2) Being 'born-again" is to be indwelt by the holiness of Jehovah. It is by His Spirit of Holiness that we become alive eternally. Just as God will never die, so those who are born again by God's Spirit will also live forever. When Jesus appeared to his disciples after his resurrection, he said, "**But you will receive power when the Holy Spirit comes upon you. And you will be My witnesses.**" (Acts 1:8) The "power" spoken of here is the root word for what we today call "dynamite." The Holy Spirit gives us the power and ability to do what we could not possibly do without Him. He "sanctifies" us. He cleanses us from sinful behaviors. It is not enough to call upon Jesus to save us. We must call upon Him in sincerity and with an attitude of conviction and with an understanding of our need for repentance. "**Not everyone who says to me, 'Lord, Lord,' will enter the kingdom of heaven, but only the one who does the will of my Father who is in heaven.**" (Matt 7:21) -- **For he who sows to his flesh will of the flesh reap corruption, but he who sows to the Spirit will of the Spirit reap everlasting life.** (Galatians 6:8)

The two unfortunate things about the Christian Church today are our lack of trust in the love of God and, our absolute need for repentance. Neither can exist without the other. It is only when we have been broken by God's overwhelming love for us, confessed our sins, solemnly sworn our allegiance to Him, and seek to live for God's pleasure and not our own that we truly experience the peace of our eternal salvation. Our relationship with God is a day by day decision. His promises are for those that patiently endure until the end. "Once saved, always saved." This is frequently said by many Christians. It is not scripturally accurate. People who were Christians, throughout the history of the Church, have changed their minds and renounced Him. Also, many have turned their backs and gone back into the world. This statement ignores one's absolute need for repentance. Its gives believers no incentive to walk in the Spirit. "**If we deliberately keep on sinning after we have received the knowledge of the truth, no sacrifice for sins is left, but only a fearful expectation of judgment and of raging fire that will consume the enemies of God.**" (Hebrews 10:23)

Therefore, even though this Psalm is short, it is also immensely powerful. In language that no one can misunderstand, we are told how to behave as children of God. It reminds us of the "fruit of the Spirit" -- "**The fruit of the Spirit is love, joy, peace, forbearance, kindness, goodness, faithfulness, gentleness and self-control. Against such things there is no law.**" (Galatians 5:22-23) Jesus explains that we can know whether someone is truly a Christian by the "fruit of the Spirit" evident in their lives. Jesus testifies that those who "*abide*" in Christ "*will bear much fruit.*" This spiritual fruit bears forbearance, patience, endurance, resilience, and longsuffering. It speaks of the ability God gives us to hold on to Him throughout our lives, despite any heartbreak, trial, tribulation, or persecution. -- This is a product of the Holy Spirit, and the "fruit" and evidence of our salvation.

In this Psalm David lists the fruit of the Spirit, using different words that also have the same purpose, to set the Path of Life straight before us. "*He who walks with integrity, and works righteousness, and speaks truth in his heart. He does not slander with his tongue, nor does evil to his neighbor, nor takes up a reproach against his friend; in whose eyes a reprobate is despised, but who honors those who fear the Lord; he swears to his own hurt and does not change; he does not put out his money at interest, nor does he take a bribe against the innocent. He who does these things will never be shaken."* (verses 2–5) This is a description of a person who has their heart and their mind aligned to achieve God's purpose. They live a life in obedience and reverence to our Maker.

We now live in the last days of this earth. We live in the 'Age of Tolerance,' when every sin and perverted imagination of mankind is not only permitted, but also celebrated. Perversion and sexual promiscuity are encouraged, just as in the days of Sodom and Gomorrah. And just as those cities practiced abominations and were destroyed, so shall our earth be destroyed too. **"The same thing will happen as occurred in the days of Lot: They were eating, drinking, buying, selling, planting, and building; but on the day that Lot went out from Sodom fire and brimstone rained from heaven and destroyed them all."** (Luke 17:28–29)

This is God's exhortation for Christians in these times, **"And do this, understanding the present time: The hour has already come for you to wake up from your slumber, because our salvation is nearer now than when we first believed. The night is nearly over; the day is almost here. So, let us put aside the deeds of darkness and put on the armor of light. Let us behave decently, as in the daytime, not in carousing and drunkenness, not in sexual immorality and debauchery, not in dissension and jealousy. Rather, clothe yourselves with the Lord Jesus Christ, and do not think about how to gratify the desires of the flesh."** (Romans 13:11–14)

We must develop "self-control" and stop seeking to gratify our personal wants and needs. This can only occur when we make the decision to die to the desires of our flesh and to live by the motivation and power of God's Holy Spirit. We must all be born-again! ***"Clothe yourselves with the Lord Jesus Christ, and do not think about how to gratify the desires of the flesh."*** (Romans 13:14)

Psalm 16

"**K**eep me safe, my God, for in you I take refuge." (verse 1) When our loving Maker hears anyone make this plea, his heart is moved to act on their behalf. How much Jehovah longs to hear this! He longs for us to run to Him and find shelter. Just as Jesus sat opposite Jerusalem and wept, "**How often I have longed to gather your children together, as a hen gathers her chicks under her wings.**" (Matthew 23:37)

Our Lord gave another example of how He reacts when anyone comes to Him for help in his parable of the "Prodigal Son." When the prodigal son's father saw his rebellious son from far away returning home, he did not wait. The father ran to meet his repentant son. "**While he was still a long way off, his father saw him and was filled with compassion for him; he ran to his son, threw his arms around him and kissed him.**" (Luke 15:20) So does our heavenly Father, as soon as we repent (turn around), and come back to Him. -- No one ever needs to be afraid of our merciful God. Even one of the criminals who perished on a cross next to Jesus that deserved the punishment of death, received mercy and forgiveness. When he asked, Jesus replied to him, "**Truly I say to you, today you shall be with Me in Paradise.**" (Luke 23:43) His promise has always been, "**Come near to God and he will come near to you. Humble yourselves before the Lord, and he will lift you up.**" (James 4:8 &10)

"*You are my Lord; apart from you I have no good thing.*" (verse 2) It is vitally important that we always have our eyes and heart open to see the multitude of blessings God pours upon us every day. In response, we should open our mouths and praise Him for His bountiful loving kindnesses. When we do this, we experience the peace, strength, and joy He promises to those that do so. This is the constant lesson that God's Spirit teaches: "**Every good and perfect gift is from above, coming down from the Father of the heavenly lights, who does not change like shifting shadows.**" (James 1:17)

God in incapable of sin. He is the embodiment of pure holiness. He is Light, and He is Life. Only God and God alone is worthy of our worship. Therefore, even when we go through fiery storms in this life, we still rejoice and praise our Lord. What crushes others does not crush us. Jesus turns our hurts and horrible experiences into things of value and worth to us and to others. This is amazing and wonderful! No matter what we experience in this world, Jehovah knows, sees, and cares. The Maker and Sustainer of the cosmos loves us. We are His children. He will help us to survive and become stronger, despite anything this fallen world throws at us. That is why the apostle Paul urges us to "**Rejoice in the Lord always. I will say it again: Rejoice! Let your gentleness be evident to all.**

The Lord is near. Do not be anxious about anything, but in every situation, by prayer and petition, with thanksgiving, present your requests to God. And the peace of God, which transcends all understanding, will guard your hearts and your minds in Christ Jesus. (Philippians 4:4–7) To react in this manner is not natural. Others may think we have gone mad. How can we suffer and rejoice? Who does this? In fact, no one can truly do this apart from the indwelling of God's Spirit. Christ has called us out of this world. We are no longer to behave in 'normal' and 'natural' ways. Instead, Christians are to be supernatural. This is our calling. This is the work of God in us.

"I say of the holy people who are in the land, "They are the noble ones in whom is all my delight." (verse 3) Those of us who have been so immensely fortunate to have received God's free gift of eternal life through the sacrifice and resurrection of His Son, are now unified in a way that no other person on earth knows, nor can understand. Daily, we remind ourselves that we are no longer our own; but we have been bought with the precious blood of the Holy One. It truly is too wonderful to even begin to understand. But someday, when Christ returns and calls us up to be with Him, we will finally see our wonderful and glorious Savior face to face. **"Now we see only a reflection as in a mirror; then we shall see face to face. Now I know in part; then I shall know fully, even as I am fully known."** (1 Corinthians 13:12)

This is how Jesus describes our relationship as Christians to God: "**I am in my Father, and you are in me, and I am in**

you." (John 14:20) This is a truth that we should think about before we begin each day. If we are indeed one with God and Christ, how then should we behave and speak to eachother? -- My wife and I lived on a mountain once near a lake surrounded by a forest of Juniper Pines. These are amazing trees that show us what this verse means. Over time, as these trees drop their cones, 3 little trees will grow near each other. Their circumference begins as spindly, little sprouts. But over the decades as they grow into tall trees, the three trees grow closer and closer together as their girths expand. Then they begin to intertwine and enmesh themselves around each other until there is only one large and very wide tree. The 3 trees become 1 mighty tree and share the same roots! Inside of all Believers resides the Holy Spirit of God. And just like these trees, as we continue to grow in the Lord, the Spirit joins us closer and closer, until we become one with eachother, sharing our mutual roots that drink daily from the infinite well of Living water provided by Jesus Christ, our God! "**I pray that all of them may be one, Father, just as you are in me and I am in you. May they also be in us so that the world may believe that you have sent me.**" (John 17:21)

"*Lord, you alone are my portion and my cup; you make my lot secure.*" (verse 5) Our victory over suffering and death happened on the Cross of Christ. It is there that the barrier between us, and our Holy God was removed. The Holy One of Heaven took upon Himself all your sins and mine. Then, he paid the penalty we could not afford. He died and suffered the penalty of our sins in our place. He did this to save all those who will accept His divine gift. Just as Christ rose from the dead to be with the Father, so we will too. -- This is the great mystery of the universe. And it is the duty of every believer to live in a way that reveals our intimate relationship with God. If we refuse to repent, then our faith is not real. We are deceiving ourselves. It is easy to tell the difference between a caterpillar and a butterfly. God is not fooled. Our lot in life will never be "*secure*" without true faith in our Maker, who loves us, and who has given His Son to suffer death in our place. "**God, our Savior, wants all people to be saved and to come to a knowledge of the truth. For there is one God and one mediator between God and man-kind, the man Christ Jesus, who gave himself as a ransom for all people**." (1 Timothy 2:3–6)

The treasures that we receive when we put our faith in Christ to save us from death are too wonderful for us to imagine. "**Eye has not seen, nor ear heard, nor have entered into the heart of man the things which God has prepared for those who love Him.**" (I Corinthians 2:9) We read his promises of what we will receive but they are far too glorious and wonderful for any human to comprehend. Whatever we imagine, it does not even begin to comprehend the glorious and beautiful rewards that we shall receive when we see Him face to face. "**Now we see only a reflection as in a mirror; then we shall see face to face. Now I know in part; then I shall know fully, even as I am fully known.**" (! Corinthians 13:12) That is the reason that David declared in this Psalm: "***The boundary lines have fallen for me in pleasant places; surely I have a delightful inheritance.***" (verse 6)

Now, David confidently proclaims his faith in God's promises. He speaks of living forever in the presence of God, in a body that will never age or decay. "*Therefore my heart is glad and my tongue rejoices; my body also will rest secure, because you will not abandon me to the realm of the dead, nor will you let your faithful one see decay.*" (verses 9–10) Just as Jesus rose from the dead in a new and far more powerful and glorious body, so we will be raised too, if we persevere in our faith until the end. – This verse can also be heard as the voice of Christ, who is truly the only "***faithful one.***" As he rose from the dead, so shall all we who believe in Him.

Despite whatever trials, tribulations, hardships, and heartbreaks that we suffer, we endure them patiently and without complaint because we have certainty of our future. We are able to experience a joy that unbelievers cannot know because the Spirit of God within us. Therefore, David sings, "***Makes known to me the path of life; you will fill me with joy in your presence, with eternal pleasures at your right hand.***" (verse 11)

"*I keep my eyes always on the Lord. With him at my right hand, I will not be shaken.*" (verse 8) This simple verse should be our daily plan and purpose. We must begin each day by directing our eyes, heart, and mind towards God through praise, prayer and reading the Bible. It is our "**daily bread**." (Matthew 6:11) Allow this final verse to be branded into our hearts and minds so that we never forget.

Psalm 17

David comes before the Lord whenever he is oppressed, depressed, or attacked by "evil men." David knows that the Lord hears him. That knowledge is David's confidence and strength. "*Hear me, Lord, my plea is just; listen to my cry.*" (verse 1)

"*Let my vindication come from you; may your eyes see what is right. Though you probe my heart, though you examine me at night and test me, you will find that I have planned no evil.*" (verses 2–3) Regardless of what others think, or even what we think of ourselves, the Lord will judge the intent of our heart. Often, our best plans to do good fail. Perhaps, we wanted to be a better person, parent, spouse, or had plans to do great things. But then life, outside influences, or our own defects of character prevented us from accomplishing those things. God knows the plans we have in our heart. Our sacrifices and efforts will not go unrewarded. When David says, "*I have planned no evil,*"

"*I call on you, my God, for you will answer me; turn your ear to me and hear my prayer. Show me the wonders of your great love, you who save by your right hand those who take refuge in you from their foes.*" (verse 6–7) As long as we continue to call on the Lord, and seek his forgiveness and help, he will listen and save us by His great love. Our "foes" are not only men of this world. Our enemies also include the Prince of this world, Lucifer (Satan), and the selfish desires of our mortal flesh. Do not judge ourselves too harshly. Many of us have inherited defects that Satan's minions use to make our struggle against sin particularly difficult, frustrating, and filled with failure. "***They have tracked me down, they now surround me, with eyes alert, to throw me to the ground. They are like a lion hungry for prey, like a fierce lion crouching in cover.***" (verse 11–12) God sees and understands far more than we do. Just continue to "**Take your stand against the devil's schemes. For our struggle is not against flesh and blood, but against the rulers, against the authorities, against the powers of this dark world, and against the spiritual forces of evil in heavenly realms.**" (Ephesians 6:11–12)

David's prayer is for God to preserve him and to keep him on the Godly way. In this psalm he is not railing against any specific enemy, but against anything that might derail him from keeping his feet from straying from the path of righteousness. "***Keep me as the apple of your eye; hide me in the shadow of your wings, from the wicked who are out to destroy me, from my mortal enemies who surround me.***" (verse 8) The "***apple of our eye***" refers to our pupils from which we see, in the center of our eyes. God put them beneath our foreheads, sheltered by bone and the shadow of our brows. In like manner David, and we too, are always to be seeking to remain in the "***shelter***" of God, beneath His brows, as the apples of His eyes.

"Arise, O Lord, confront him, bring him low; deliver my soul from the wicked with Your sword, from men with Your hand, O Lord, from men of the world, whose portion is in this life." (verses 13–14B) The Holy Scriptures reveals the contrast between the wicked who do not consider eternity, and those who take refuge in the Lord. This difference should be evident in every Believer. Followers of Christ do not seek after the enticements and comforts that this world offers. In fact, we disdain them. **"Anyone who chooses to be a friend of the world becomes an enemy of God."** (James 4:4) We see the life we now live to be temporary. It is a brief time that our Maker gives us to live in this flesh. It is given to us for one primary purpose: To choose between Life or Death. Those who seek after the things of this world and oppress and deal falsely with others will not inherit eternal life. They will die like everything else on this planet. But that will not be their end, as they suppose. They have chosen to be ignorant of accepting the truth of the Holy Word. They have ignored the fact that all humans are made in God's image and possess eternal souls. **"And the Lord God formed man of the dust of the ground and breathed into his nostrils the breath of life: and man became a living soul."** (Gen. 2:7). Therefore, they will not enter into the Paradise that God has prepared for those who love Him. Nor, as they may hope, will they die and go into unconscious oblivion. They will live on forever; but, in darkness and immense misery because they chose to believe and trust in the things of this world, instead of its Maker and Savior.

David ends his psalm by declaring what faithful believers in Jesus Christ will receive. We will be declared righteous when we rise from death to see and to be with the Lord forever. "*As for me, I will be vindicated and will see your face; when I awake, I will be satisfied with seeing your likeness.*" (verse 15) Believers do not live their lives here seeking after things in this world that make us happy and content temporarily. We take this short life very seriously. It determines where we shall spend forever. Our constant hope is to see Jesus when we awake from death.

Psalm 18

"*I love you, Lord, my strength.*" (verse 1) The most wonderful words that any parent can hear from their children are these: "*I love you.*" (verse 1) When our children say these words our hearts flood with kindness towards them. It is also true with our God.

The apostle John began his time with Jesus as a "**son of thunder**;" (Mark 3:17) but, as he grew in the Spirit, he became known as the 'Apostle of Love.' "**Beloved, let us love one another, for love is from God, and whoever loves has been born of God and knows God.**" (1 John 4:7) The "love" that God possesses and gives to us is far different from the love that the unbelieving, worldly person feels. The most true and perfect "**love is from God.**" (1 John 4:8) This is pure and undefiled love. It does not change. It is always true and faithful. The love God gives to believers is described thusly: "**Love is patient, love is kind. It does not envy, it does not boast, it is not proud. It does not dishonor others, it is not self-seeking, it is not easily angered, it keeps no record of wrongs. Love does not delight in evil but rejoices with the truth. It always protects, always trusts, always hopes, always perseveres. Love never fails.**" (1 Corinthians 13:4–8)

Nowhere has the love of God been revealed to us more than in the person of Jesus and the life that he lived, and then gave up for our salvation. **"By this we know love, that he laid down his life for us, and we ought to lay down our lives for the brothers."** (1 John 3:16–18) When any person sincerely comes before God in the name of Jesus with a humble and broken spirit and asks for Him to forgive their sins and to accept them as a child of God, this is the love of God that they receive. **"If God is for us, no one can defeat us. He did not spare his own Son but gave him for us all. So, with Jesus, God will surely give us all things…Yes, I am sure that neither death, nor life, nor angels, nor ruling spirits, nothing now, nothing in the future, no powers, nothing above us, nothing below us, nor anything else in the whole world will ever be able to separate us from the love of God that is in Christ Jesus our Lord."** (Romans 8:31–32 & 38–39)

"The LORD is my rock and my fortress and my deliverer, my God, my rock, in whom I take refuge, my shield, and the horn of my salvation, my stronghold." (verse 2) David describes the everlasting strength of God's love as immovable and permanent. David also claims that God is our strength, and refuge. For believers, God is our security and peace because we are certain of His love for us.

"In my distress I called to the Lord; I cried to my God for help. From his temple he heard my voice; my cry came before him, into his ears." (verse 6) Regardless of any circumstance that we encounter, we know that the Maker of all that is seen and unseen, the God of Love, is on our side. We know Him through

His Son, Jesus Christ, who has nail holes in His hands and feet. It is the Spirit of Christ that spoke these words: "**Can a woman forget her nursing child, or lack compassion for the son of her womb? Though she may forget, I will not forget you! "Behold, I have inscribed you on the palms of My hands; your walls are ever before Me.**" (Isaiah 49:16) The inscription Christ refers to on his palms are the nail holes from hanging on his cross. Therefore, we never need to be afraid of Jesus forgetting us. We can have that same surety and confidence that David had. God loves us and listens when we call to Him.

From verses 7 through 15 the psalmist waxes poetic and uses metaphors to explain how quickly and powerfully Jehovah came to his rescue. "***He mounted the cherubim and flew; he soared on the wings of the wind.***" (verse 10) Then, David testifies about God's deliverance: "***He sent from on high, He took me; He drew me out of many waters. He delivered me from my strong enemy, and from those who hated me, for they were too mighty for me. They confronted me in the day of my calamity, but the Lord was my stay. He brought me forth also into a broad place; He rescued me, because He delighted in me.***" (verses 16–19) God hears us when we speak to Him. He lifts us up and out of our troubles. And he sets us in a place out of reach from our enemies. He is indeed our deliverer because Jehovah is truly "***delighted***" with us. We receive the eternal help and unending love of our Maker through our acceptance of God's free gift. "**For it is by grace you have been saved, through faith—and this is not from yourselves, it is the gift of God— not by works, so that no one can boast.**" (Ephesians 2:8–9)

David makes claims that God always answers his prayers and protects him because "***The Lord has rewarded me according to my righteousness.***" (verse 20) When we make the choice to live as our Creator desires, instead of how we want, then we are choosing to be on God's side and in his family. This is the only righteousness that we can give to God: our willingness to follow in his ways rather than our own. For as the Apostle James writes, "**You believe that there is one God. You do well. Even the demons believe—and tremble! But do you want to know, O foolish man, that faith without works is dead?**" (James 2:19–20) We cannot fool God by saying we believe but not making any changes in the way we think, speak, and act. The Good News is not just mentally agreeing that Christ in God's Son. Demons know this much! Anyone who claims to be a follower of Jesus Christ is inevitably a new person. We do not behave as unbelievers do. Yes, we slip-up sometimes, perhaps even often; but we always get back up, confess our sins, and get back on the Path of Life. We practice seeking after God and his righteousness. We do not quit doing so, despite how often we might fail. "**For if we confess our sins, he is faithful and just and will forgive us our sins and purify us from all unrighteousness.**" (1 John 1:9)

It is not easy to be a Christian. Being a Christian is not a one-time confession. It is a daily effort. It requires us to use our free will and to choose God over ourselves. David was "Christian" because he believed in God's Son and lived to please his Maker more than himself. Therefore, David can say, "*I was also blameless with Him, and I kept myself from my iniquity. Therefore, the Lord has recompensed me according to my righteousness, according to the cleanness of my hands in His eyes."* (verses 23–24) God declares us to be "**blameless**" when we hold fast to Him through faith.

If we desire to receive God's kindness and blessings, then we must treat others in the same way as we want to be treated. Therefore, David says, *"With the kind You show Yourself kind; with the blameless You show Yourself blameless; with the pure You show Yourself pure, and with the crooked You show Yourself astute. For You save an afflicted people, but haughty eyes You abase* (humiliate). *For You light my lamp; the Lord my God illumines my darkness."* (verses 25–28)

David continues to praise the Lord for his many mercies. It is indeed a song of love and thankfulness to his heavenly Defender. *"The Lord lives! Praise be to my Rock! Exalted be God my Savior! He is the God who avenges me, who subdues nations under me, who saves me from my enemies. You exalted me above my foes; from a violent man you rescued me."* (verses 46–48)

In return for His unending love, the Lord asks so little of us. Continuously throughout the Bible, and especially in these Psalms, David is always telling us to join Him in praising God. The person whose heart and mouth are always declaring God's goodness overcomes the world and sin. That person "**walks in the Spirit and does not fulfill the desires of the flesh.**" (Galatians 5:16)

David closes by fulfilling the purpose of the Holy Spirit who inspired him to write this praise of God for his abundant mercy, love, and kindness. *"Therefore, I will give thanks to You among the nations, O' Lord, and I will sing praises to Your name. He gives great deliverance to His king, and shows lovingkindness to His anointed, to David and his descendants forever."* (verses 49–50)

Psalm 19

When I read this psalm, I think of David as a shepherd boy looking up at the starry night. "*The heavens declare the glory of God; the skies proclaim the work of his hands.*" (verse 1) David claims that the natural world informs us about the nature of God, the Creator, just by looking up at the heavens. "*Day after day they pour forth speech; night after night they reveal knowledge.*" (verse 2) He uses our Sun as an illustration: "*It rises at one end of the heavens and makes its circuit to the other; nothing is deprived of its warmth.*" (verse 6) God blesses both the innocent and the guilty every day. "**God causes his sun to rise on the evil and the good; and he sends rain on the righteous and the unrighteous.**" (Matthew 5:45)

When we look up at the wonders of the night sky, we realize how minute and seemingly insignificant we are. In the pictures that our satellite observatories are giving us, we discover that there are more galaxies than grains of sand on all the beaches of the world! Plus, millions more are being created every day. -- Naturally, from our earliest ancestors until now we ask, "Out the immensity of all God's creation, why does he care about me?"

As we move further into the 21st Century, there has been a rapid increase of people who deny the existence of God. Largely, this is due to our public school system that teaches that creation is an "accident." Our children are taught from the time they go to school that all that is seen and unseen is the result of billions of years of 'random, chaotic elements colliding together' until everything fit into perfect harmony and the first micro-organisms were made, from which all life has 'evolved.' David disputes this.

In verse 7–10, we are told that the "***knowledge***" that "***the heavens declare, and the skies proclaim,***" are "***laws, statutes, precepts and decrees,***" that God has set in place to maintain all of creation's wonders. All of God's works are "***perfect, trustworthy, right, and firm.***" (verses 7–9) In the Bible's last book, Revelation, we hear ourselves before His throne saying, "**Worthy are you, our Lord and God, the Holy One, to receive the glory, ... for thou hast created all things, and for thy pleasure they are created.**" (Revelation 4:11)

"***The fear of the Lord is pure, enduring forever.***" (verse 9) When we recognize the majestic, awesome power of God, our first impulse is "***fear.***" It is a good thing to be afraid of offending the righteous God. Solomon, David's son wrote, "**The fear of the LORD is the beginning of wisdom, and knowledge of the Holy One is understanding.**" (Proverbs 9:10)

Knowing what pleases God and what does not and making a firm decision to behave in ways that make Him happy, is plain and simple wisdom. Children know this about their parents. It makes sense that we should know this about our Heavenly

Parent too. In fact, Paul says that when we are born we all have the knowledge of God. It is innate. As long as we breathe and have life, this knowledge is always with us. **"For since the creation of the world God's invisible qualities—his eternal power and divine nature—have been clearly seen, being understood from what has been made, so that people are without excuse."** (Romans 1:20)

How did mankind come to fear God in the first place? It began in the Garden when Adam and Eve chose to obey Satan, rather than their Maker. **"You will not certainly die," the serpent said to the woman. "For God knows that when you eat from it your eyes will be opened, and you will be like God, knowing good and evil."** (Genesis 3:4–5) Of course, soon afterwards, both the man and the woman were thrown out of the Garden and ever since hardships have been the destiny of every human being. Therefore, it is wise to **"fear the Lord."**

David wants to be certain that there is nothing he says or does that offends Jehovah. David knows that God is with the upright. He sees the rules of human behavior that God has decreed as wisdom from above to be followed. David knew that those who obey are blessed; and those that do not obey are punished. He made a choice to live according to God's rules. ***"More to be desired are they than gold, yea, than much fine gold: sweeter also than honey and the honeycomb. Moreover, by them is thy servant warned: and in keeping of them there is great reward."*** (verses 10–11)

Do not be become discouraged that we must continue to discipline our flesh and wrestle against unwanted desires. It is a part of the "curse" of knowing good from evil. Like David, come before the Lord, with thanksgiving, and in humble contrition. Let us in deepest sincerity also pray these words: "*Forgive my hidden faults. Keep your servant also from willful sins; may they not rule over me. Then I will be blameless, innocent of great transgression. May these words of my mouth and this meditation of my heart be pleasing in your sight, Lord, my Rock and my Redeemer.*" (verse 12–13)

Psalm 20

This psalm recites the prayer of King David for his people, particularly before going into battle. "*May the name of the Lord answer you when you are in distress; may the name of the God of Jacob protect you.*" (verse 1) We all have battles. Life is filled with them. We all have days of "*distress.*"

The phrase "*in the name of the Lord*" is repeated as a refrain in verses 1, 5, and 7 for emphasis. And in verse 2 it is mentioned again. "*May the name of the God of Jacob set you securely on high and defend you in battle!*" Knowing "*the name of God*" is vitally important! There are myriads of gods that humanity worships; but they are the products of mankind's imagination.

The primary tenet of Judaism is said by Moses, "**Hear, O Israel: The Lord our God is one Lord!**" (Deuteronomy 6:4) Moses explains the importance for us to know and believe this: "**You shall not follow other gods, any of the gods of the peoples who surround you, for the Lord your God in the midst of you is a jealous God; otherwise the anger of the Lord your God will be kindled against you, and He will wipe you off the face of the earth.**" (Deuteronomy 64:14 -15)

Jesus is the Holy Son of the trinity. He is "one with the Father." The prophet Isaiah said, "**And he will be called Wonderful Counselor, Mighty God, Everlasting Father, Prince of Peace.**" (Isaiah 9:6) Jesus is our God. He is named in the Old Testament and in the New Testament: "**Thus says the LORD, the King and Redeemer of Israel, the LORD of Hosts: "I am the first and I am the last, and there is no God but Me."** (Isaiah 44:6)

We must frequently meditate upon and consider the immensity, power, wisdom, and blessings of the one and only God, "*the God of Jacob.*" (verse 1) Repeatedly, we are asked to think deeply about the God who "*sets us securely on high, who grants our heart's desire and fulfills all our counsel, who gives us victory, fulfill all our petitions, and saves us.*" (verses 4–7)

Solomon, who was given more wisdom than any man, instructs us, "**As a man thinketh in his heart, so is he.**" (Proverbs 23:7) If we are to be God's people then we must take time every day to think about Him and His ways.

Jacob was the grandson of Abraham. "**God said to him, "Your name is Jacob, but you will no longer be called Jacob; your name will be Israel." So, he named him Israel. And God said to him, "I am God Almighty; be fruitful and increase in number. A nation and a community of nations will come from you, and kings will be among your descendants."** (Genesis 35:9) -- This is vital for all Christians to understand: All believers in Christ are the descendants of Abraham and Jacob. We are the people of the heavenly Israel. We are the descendants that God has chosen from among the nations. All who have the same faith in God as Abraham will inherit all of God's promises given to Abraham and Israel (Jacob). Now, we who were not born as Jews, also have been declared to be the children of God's promises. We receive the gift of righteousness in the same way that Abraham did, "**We believe in the God of Abraham and Jacob, and it is accounted** (to us) **as righteousness.**" (Romans 4:2) Be confidently assured that all the promises and blessings in the Bible belong to us who believe, who are not Jews by the flesh, but by the faith given to us by being "born-again" through the indwelling of God's Spirit. We too are the "children of Abraham" by sharing the same faith in the same God.

This is a psalm that David and his people recited before going into battle. "*Some boast in chariots and some in horses, but we will boast in the name of our God. They have bowed down and fallen, but we have risen and stood upright. Save, o' Lord; may the King answer us when we call.*" (verse 7–9) David's purpose was to remind the people that God is their strength and their confidence. Therefore, in our "*day of trouble*" (verse 1) we can recite this psalm with David and God's people throughout the ages. Know for certain that all sinners who humble themselves in reverence to the one and only God will be heard, because Jesus is ours, and we are His. Our God will "*defend, strengthen, and remember our heart's desire, and fulfill all our plans.*" (verse 4)

Psalm 21

In every psalm one can find lines and themes that apply to Christ; for, every word that David wrote was chosen by the Holy Spirit of Christ. Far more than any prophet before him, David revealed things about God's plan for our redemption that extended from David's days until eternity. This is one of those psalms. We can read this psalm as referring to Christ, the Messiah and King of Kings.

In Psalm 21, David foresees the coming of Jehovah as the Messiah and Savior of all mankind, Jesus Christ. "***O Lord, in Your strength the king will be glad, and in Your salvation how greatly he will rejoice!***" (verse 1) David uses "***Your and he***," which indicates that David is speaking about another person other than himself as being the "***King***."

It took tremendous "***strength***" for Jesus the man to submit to dying on a cross. He sweat blood while pleading with His Father, "**If there be any other way, let this cup pass from me.**" (Matthew 26:39) But Jesus concluded this same prayer with, "**Nevertheless, not my will, but yours be done.**" (Luke 22:42) The Father gave Jesus the strength he needed to accomplish the greatest deed ever done on earth. If Jesus had not obeyed, died, and then risen from the dead, then all would be lost. As Paul says, "**If the dead are not raised, then "let us eat and drink, for tomorrow we die**." (1 Corinthians 15:22) Before his crucifixion, Pilate asked Jesus if he were indeed a king. His answer said it all: "**I was born and came into the world for this one purpose.**" (John 18:37)

The Son of God stepped down from his throne in heaven to die and pay the penalty of death for the sins that we all have committed. It was necessary for Christ to rise from the dead, so that those who believe in and follow Him, will rise from the dead too. This is why the king is "*glad*" and "*rejoices!*" We have been made God's eternal sons and daughters through Christ. "**But we do see Jesus, who was made lower than the angels for a little while, now crowned with glory and honor because he suffered death, so that by the grace of God he might taste death for everyone. In bringing many sons and daughters to glory, it was fitting that God, for whom and through whom everything exists, should make the pioneer of their salvation perfect through what he suffered. Both the one who makes people holy and those who are made holy are of the same family. So, Jesus is not ashamed to call them brothers and sisters. He says, "I will declare your name to my brothers and sisters; in the assembly I will sing your praises.**" (Hebrews 2:9–12)

"*You have given him his heart's desire, and You have not withheld the request of his lips. Selah.*" (verse 2) In the purest translations, verse 2 ends with the word "*Selah.*" This means that David wants us to stop and think about what he just wrote.

-- What is our Lord's "***desire***" and his "***request***"? We are given this answer in John **"After Jesus said this, he looked toward heaven and prayed, "Father, the hour has come. Glorify your Son, that your Son may glorify you. For you granted him authority over all people that he might give eternal life to all those you have given him. Now this is eternal life: that they know you, the only true God, and Jesus Christ, whom you have sent, so that he might give eternal life.** (John 17:1-3) -- The first request of Jesus is that we "**know God and Jesus Christ, whom you have sent.**" (John 17:3)

Our Lord's second request is: "**And now, Father, glorify me in your presence with the glory I had with you before the world began.**" (John 17:5) David foresees the Father answering this prayer of the coming King, "*His glory is great through your salvation, splendor and majesty You place upon him. For You make him most blessed forever; You make him joyful with gladness in Your presence.*" (verses 5–6)

Our Lord's third request for us is: "**I will remain in the world no longer, but they are still in the world, and I am coming to you. Holy Father, protect them by the power of your name, the name you gave me, so that they may be one as we are one.**" (John 17:11) Divisions and quarrels among Christians should never be. We are always to "**love one another**" (John 13:34) as our Lord commands. Just as there is unity with the Father and the Son, so too it is to be with us. We are united to the Holy Trinity!

"*For the king trusts in the* LORD, *and through the lovingkindness of the Most High he will not be shaken.*" (verse 7) The earth and all who are in it will be **shaken** when experiencing the difficult times that are coming before Jesus returns. The rest of this psalm refers what is coming in our time. "*Your hand will find out all your enemies; your right hand will find out those who hate you. You will make them as a fiery oven in the time of your anger; the Lord will swallow them up in His wrath, and fire will devour them. Their offspring You will destroy from the earth, and their descendants from among the sons of men. Though they intended evil against You and devised a plot, they will not succeed. For You will make them turn their back; You will aim with Your bowstrings at their faces.*" (verses 8–12)

We have filled our streets with the blood of war and violence. Starvation and the oppression of the poor occurs all across the world. But perhaps worse of all is what we have done to the earth itself. We have polluted it to such an extent with our careless and selfish lifestyles that the earth is dying. We have made our own planet unlivable! We have cut down our forests, polluted our waters, and filled the air with poison. Earth's resources have been stripped and used to make a few rich, and to fuel our materialistic desires. Those who are supposed to be the wisest and most trustworthy among us to lead, are corrupt. They are rich men who participate in the destruction of war, pollution, and the oppression of the poor.

Throughout the bible and David's psalms, we read about the day of God's punishment for the sinfulness of mankind. "**For he has set a day when he will judge the world with justice by the man he has appointed.**" (Acts 17:31) The time of our

Lord's judgement is here. This is the last generation on earth. When Jesus was asked about what the signs of the End will be, one of the things He told us to look for was the re-establishment of the nation Israel. The Lord claimed, "**I say to you, this generation will not pass away until all these come to pass.**" (Matthew 24:34) This warning is repeated with additional information throughout the Old and the New Testaments.

Jesus emphasized that we must always be ready for his return to lift His Church off the earth before the Tribulation occurs. We are strongly instructed to "**be on the alert**" for these signs. "**Take heed, keep on the alert; for you do not know when the appointed time will come. It is like a man away on a journey, who upon leaving his house and putting his slaves in charge, assigning to each one his task, also commanded the doorkeeper to stay on the alert. Therefore, be on the alert—for you do not know when the master of the house is coming, whether in the evening, at midnight, or when the rooster crows, or in the morning— in case he should come suddenly and find you asleep. What I say to you I say to all, 'Be on the alert!'**" (Mark 13:33–37)

"*Be exalted, O Lord, in Your strength; we will sing and praise Your power.*" (verse 13) True believers in God "*exalt*" Him. We honor the Lord before all others and things. He is supreme above us. He is holy. He is wise. He is the embodiment of pure love. "***His glory is great; you have bestowed on him splendor and majesty.***" (verse 5) Our Maker, who loves us and sustains us, commands respect. We are to put our entire life into His hands. Just as Jesus trusts in the Father, we are to entrust ourselves and our decisions to God also. "***For the king trusts in the LORD; through the unfailing love of the Most High he will not be shaken.***" (verse 7) This is how we succeed in life and find purpose, happiness, and peace. We honor God by trusting Him and following in His footsteps.

Psalm 22

In this psalm David prophetically recites the thoughts and words of Christ when crucified! It is proof of David's inspiration from God. No man could have written what would happened to Jesus 1,400 years in the future with these specific details. Prophetic passages like this are throughout the Bible. They are proof of the veracity of the prophets and apostles who wrote them. Any rational, objective, person who reads the Bible with an open mind, would have to agree that prophecies in the Bible have been fulfilled exactly as they were spoken. How else can this be explained, except that the writers of the Bible spoke by the Spirit of the Living God, for whom there is no past nor present?

"My God, my God, why have you forsaken me?" (verse 1 & Matthew 27:46)) There is great significance in this utterance. It represents the most important event in human history. This testifies to the very moment when your sins and mine were laid upon our Savior and Redeemer. "**For He made Him who knew no sin to be sin for us, that we might become the righteousness of God in Him.**" (2 Corinthians 5:2) At the moment that Christ, the Son of God, spoke these words he became sin for us.

The apostle Matthew describes the event of Jesus' crucifixion like this: **"Now from the sixth hour darkness fell upon all the land until the ninth hour. About the ninth hour Jesus cried out with a loud voice, saying, "Eli, Eli, lama sabachthani?" that is, "My God, My God, why have You forsaken Me? ... And Jesus cried out again with a loud voice and yielded up His spirit."** (Matthew 27:45–51) Jesus died. He suffered death for you and for me, so that we do not need to do so. **"For Christ also suffered for sins once for all, the righteous for the unrighteous, to bring you to God."** (1 Peter 3:18)

Just then the temple curtain was torn in two, from top to bottom." (Matthew 27:44–51) – A very thick curtain had separated the priestly service area of the Jerusalem temple from the place where the Ark of the Covenant and the presence of God's Shekinah glory resided. Only once a year was the high priest permitted to enter into this sacred area, on the Day of Atonement, to pour the blood of an unblemished lamb on the altar between the Cherubim, whose wings sheltered the cover of the Ark. -- When Christ died for the sins of all mankind that curtain was ripped from top to bottom. The size and thickness of the curtain ensured that no one would accidentally fall into the Holy of Holies as the veil was 60 feet long, 30 feet wide, and was about one inch thick and was so massive and heavy that it took 30 priests to manipulate it so there was no way that someone could inadvertently trip and stumble into the Holy of Holies and subsequently die as a result.

No human could possibly have torn this curtain. It was an act of our loving and merciful God to show us that Jesus is now our

High Priest. He has entered the Holies of Holies and poured his own blood upon that altar in heaven. We no longer need a human priest to come before God in our place to make restitution for our sins. Now we can all go behind the curtain and have access into the Holy of Holies. **"We have confidence to enter the holy places by the blood of Jesus"** (Hebrews 10:19).

"Yet you are enthroned as the Holy One; you are the one Israel praises. In you our ancestors put their trust, and you delivered them. To you they cried out and were saved; in you they trusted and were not put to shame." (verses 3–5) This is the real theme of this psalm. We are to trust in the love and mercy of God. -- Hopefully, none of us will be crucified. But we all go through various trials and tribulations. We must trust in the love of God, revealed to us by His Holy Son, sacrificed for our sins. **"When you go through deep waters, I will be with you. When you go through rivers of difficulty, you will not drown. When you walk through the fire of oppression, you will not be burned up; the flames will not consume you."** (Isaiah 43:2)

Now David begins to describe Christ's crucifixion: *"They pierce my hands and my feet. All my bones are on display; people stare and gloat over me. They divide my clothes among them and cast lots for my garment."* (verses 16–18) These details are described so accurately in Matthew 27. They match to perfection everything David prophesied 1400 years before it happened. Knowing this, we can absolutely trust the Bible, and every word in it. It was indeed written by men who were inspired by the Holy Spirit of God. The 'Truth' that all mankind seeks is embodied in Jesus Christ.

"*He has not despised or scorned the suffering of the afflicted one; he has not hidden his face from him but has listened to his cry for help.*" (verse 24) Jesus is the "*afflicted one*" spoken of here. The prophet Isaiah, who prophecies many things about Christ's sufferings, and the establishment of His kingdom on earth, used similar language describing the events and the purpose for God's Son being crucified: "**Surely he has borne our griefs and carried our sorrows; yet we esteemed him stricken, smitten by God, and <u>afflicted</u>. But he was pierced for our transgressions; he was crushed for our iniquities; upon him was the chastisement that brought us peace, and with his wounds we are healed.**" (Isaiah 53:4–5)

Jesus' death on the Cross is the fulfillment of God's plan for redeeming mankind from our 'fall' in the Garden, when our father, Adam, and our mother, Eve, chose to disobey God in order that they could be equal to Him and know good from evil. Yes, mankind certainly knows what evil is now. It has plagued the earth and humanity ever since. In addition, when Adam submitted to Satan and obeyed him, Adam, as the representative of all mankind lost his authority over the earth, which God had given Adam to 'rule over.' Paul confirms this: "**Don't you realize that you become the slave of whatever you choose to obey?**" (Romans 6:16) Therefore Satan is now the ruler of the world, not mankind. This has been revealed to us also by the prophet Isaiah, as he describes him. "**He who is smiting peoples in wrath, a smiting without intermission, He who is ruling in anger nations, pursuing without restraint!**" (Isaiah 14:6)

Christ came first as a suffering servant. He shared our humanity and experienced the hardships and heartaches of being human. "**Surely, he hath borne our griefs, and carried our sorrows: yet we did esteem him stricken, smitten of God, and afflicted. But he was wounded for our transgressions, he was bruised for our iniquities: the chastisement of our peace was upon him; and with his stripes we are healed. All we like sheep have gone astray; we have turned everyone to his own way; and the LORD hath laid on him the iniquity of us all.**" (Isaiah 53:3) -- Christ came not only to save all who will put their trust in Him; but, also to save the earth and nature from the rule of Satan. Our new earth will be beautiful! "*Then I saw a new heaven and a new earth, for the first heaven and earth had passed away,*" (Revelation 21:1)

Not every prophecy in this psalm has yet been fulfilled. "*All the ends of the earth will remember and turn to the Lord, and all the families of the nations will worship before You. For the kingdom is the Lord's and He rules over the nations.*" (Verses 27-28) The ultimate completion of biblical prophecy will be when this promise is made real at Christ's 2nd coming. He came first as a suffering servant. He is coming again as Lord of Lords and King of Kings. "**Christ, having been offered once to bear the sins of many, will appear a second time, not to deal with sin but to save those who are eagerly waiting for him.**" (Hebrews 9:28)

When Christ returns, time and death will no longer be our reality. We will be given beautiful, brightly shining bodies that will never age, nor ever be injured, hungry or sick." (1 Corinthians

15: 52-53) This great event is referred to as the "Rapture." It gives believers hope and encouragement that helps us endure all hardships and even death: "**For we believe that Jesus died and rose again, and so we believe that God will bring with Jesus those who have fallen asleep in him. According to the Lord's word, we tell you that we who are still alive, who are left until the coming of the Lord, will certainly not precede those who have fallen asleep. For the Lord himself will come down from heaven, with a loud command, with the voice of the archangel and with the trumpet call of God, and the dead in Christ will rise first. After that, we who are still alive and are left will be caught up together with them in the clouds to meet the Lord in the air. And so, we will be with the Lord forever. Therefore encourage one another with these words.**" (1 Thessalonians 4:14-18)

"*They will come and will declare His righteousness to a people who will be born, that He has performed it.*" (verse 31) This last verse confirms the commission Jesus gave to all those who believe in Him. We are to "*declare*" that all people can receive the forgiveness of God and the "*righteousness*" of Christ. This is our marching orders for those who follow Christ. Despite all hardships we face, we are never to stop testifying that our eternal salvation is secure because Jesus Christ has "*performed it.*"

Psalm 23

This is the most read and beloved Psalm. It is quoted across the world. It paints a wonderful picture of Christ being our Shepherd. We love this psalm because of the image of Jesus as our Shepherd, and the care He has for us. Like the sheep that a shepherd owns and watches over carefully, so does our Savior watch over us. What a comfort Psalm 23 is and has been to God's sheepfold down through the ages. David had been a shepherd as a boy, hence his comparison of God caring for us as a shepherd cares for his sheep. This Psalm, like so many scriptures throughout the Bible, explains in very simple terms how much God loves us. If we believe the words of this psalm, then we will fulfill God's purposes and will. For, if we truly trust in the truth of this psalm, then we will not fear; but we will have peace, strength, and joy. The utter simplicity of God's salvation has been put into these 6 lines. Its sweetness and spirituality are unsurpassed. ***"The Lord is my shepherd"*** (verse 1) confirms to us that we are under the pastoral care of Jehovah. ***"I shall not want."*** (verse 1) This is the confidence and the trust that sheep have in their shepherd. They do not worry about what they shall eat, or how they'll be protected, or provided for. This is the faith that the Lord desires for us to have towards Him. We are to "**Trust in the Lord with all your heart and lean not on your own understanding; in all your ways acknowledge Him, And He shall direct your paths.**" (Proverbs 3:5) The Lord wants us to be calm and content, never anxious or afraid. "**Be anxious for nothing, but in everything by prayer and supplication, with thanksgiving, let your requests be made known to God; and the peace of God which surpasses all understanding, will guard your hearts and minds through Christ Jesus.**" (Philippians 4:6-7)

Know this, says the Lord, "**Do not fear, for I have redeemed you; I have called you by name; you are Mine! "When you pass through the waters, I will be with you; and through the rivers, they will not overflow you. When you walk through the fire, you will not be scorched, nor will the flame burn you. "For I am the Lord your God, the Holy One of Israel, your Savior.**" (Isaiah 43: 1-3) This is what the Lord desires for all of His sheep: Know that the Lord is for you. He is our protector and provider. We are His "beloved."

Jesus tells us, "**Don't let your heart be troubled. Believe in God; believe also in me.**" (John 14:10) And again, "**Peace I leave with you; my peace I give you. I do not give to you as the world gives. Do not let your hearts be troubled and do not be afraid.** (John 14:27) Trust in our righteous, ever loving Savior to provide all that we need. "**Seek ye first the kingdom of God.**" (Matthew 6:33) Do not worry about the things of this world and how we shall provide for ourselves and our families. Do what God has set before you to do. Do it unto the Lord, with love in your hearts. Do not complain and grumble for more. Trust in the Lord's love for us. Rejoice in what the Lord provides, and He will make us to *"lie down in green pastures; and He leads us beside still waters."* (verse 2)

"He restores my soul" (verse 3) Our souls are the spirit (essence) of who we truly are. Our bodies are temporary 'tents' for our souls. This is mysterious; but it is what the word of God teaches. **"That which is born of the flesh is flesh, and that which is born of the Spirit is spirit."** (John 3:6) There is a distinct difference between the two. Unlike our physical body, which ages, and withers until it dies, our souls are eternal.

Our bodies turn back into the dust from which they came; but our souls do not.

Simply, the souls of all mankind will spend eternity in one of two places: Heaven or Hell. Heaven is where God resides, and Hell is reserved for Satan, his fallen angels, and for those who did not seek after God. Therefore, it is imperative that we never hesitate to share about God's free gift of His righteousness through Jesus Christ. Jehovah does not want anyone's soul to perish. He loves mankind. We are the work of his hands. He created the earth and all the life upon it. He is Life. Just as He is also Love. How do we know? **"For God so loved the world that he gave his one and only Son, that whoever believes in him shall not perish but have eternal life."** (John 3:16) Hell is devoid of love, relationships, thought, knowledge, and wisdom. There is no light, and no praise of God. Its inhabitants are weak, trembling shades, who can never hope to escape from its gates. Whereas the Kingdom of God and of His Christ is so wonderfully indescribable that Paul, who was taken up to see it says, "**We declare God's wisdom, a mystery that has been hidden and that God destined for our glory before time began. None of the rulers of this age understood it, for if they had, they would not have crucified the Lord of glory. However, as it is written: "No eye has seen, nor ear has heard, nor can the human mind even conceive the things that God has prepared for those who love him."** (1 Corinthians 2:7-9) Every soul is dead already because of sin. **"Therefore, just as sin entered the world through one man, and death through sin, and in this way, death came to all people, because all sinned."** (Romans 5:12) That is the very purpose that Jesus came and died on the cross, and then came alive and rose to heaven. Jesus came to give us life. **"I have come that they may have life, and have it in all its fullness."** (John 10:10) He gave mankind His life in exchange for ours! Since sin brings death, Christ suffered death in our place. This is the Good News of true Christianity! **"I am the gate. If anyone enters through Me, he will be saved. He will come in and go out and find pasture. I am the good shepherd. The good shepherd lays down His life for the sheep."** (John 10:11) *"He guides me in the paths of righteousness for His name's sake."* (verse 3) In order for God to guide us and be our Shepherd, something must happen to us. It is absolutely necessary. No one can get to heaven without it. "Jesus answered, **"This is the absolute truth: I tell you no one can enter the kingdom of God unless they are born of water and the Spirit. Flesh gives birth to flesh, but the Spirit gives birth to spirit. You should not be surprised at my saying, '<u>You must be born again</u>.'"** (John 3:6-7) This is wonderful! How fortunate that the God of the universe loves mankind. "*He restores my soul.*" *(verse 3)* Now, we understand what this simple statement means. God brings our souls to life! This happens when we accept His Holy Son, Jesus the Christ, who gave his life as a ransom for ours. This is how our souls are "born again!"

Being born again is the most significant moment you can have in this life. For until that time, "**As for you, you were dead in your transgressions and sins, in which you used to live when you followed the ways of this world and of the ruler of the kingdom of the air, the spirit who is now at work in those who are disobedient. All of us also lived among them at one time, gratifying the cravings of our flesh and following its desires and thoughts. Like the rest, we were by nature deserving of wrath.**" (Ephesians 2:1-3) This is our state of being before receiving Christ as God's Son, who was sent to pay the price for our sins and set us free from the penalty we all deserve, death. "**But because of his great love for us, God, who is rich in mercy, made us alive with Christ even when we were dead in transgressions – it is by grace you have been saved.**" (Ephesians 2:4-5) Indeed, the love of God has "restored our souls." Once we are born-again, it is the beginning of a lifetime journey. "*He guides me in the paths of righteousness, for His name's sake.*" *(verse 3)* John Bunyan's Pilgrim's Progress is a wonderful allegorical description of our Christian walk and the trials and victories we experience as we draw nearer and nearer to God. For when the Holy Spirit comes to live within us, we begin the process of sanctification, a washing away of our sinful habits and desires, and the development of a Godly and loving character. This often takes time and requires us to be patient and to seek continually after what pleases our Maker. This is not something we can do by ourselves. God saves us and cleanses us from all sin. But it does not happen without our willingness. Jesus knocks on the door of our hearts. He never kicks the door down. We must be yielded to Him. We must humble ourselves before our Maker and seek his sanctification. Be sincerely willing to do whatever it takes to be close to Christ and to stay there. You can do it. Jesus will be with you and make sure that you stay on the Path of Life. "**Come to me, all you who are weary and burdened, and I will give you rest. Take my yoke upon you and learn from me, for I am gentle and humble in heart, and you will find rest for your souls. For my yoke is easy and my burden is light.**" (Matthew 11:28-30) And if you stray, he will come and find you and bring you back into to fellowship, when we are ready to confess our sins and repent. "**Jesus told them this parable: "Suppose one of you has a hundred sheep and loses one of them. Doesn't he leave the ninety-nine in the open country and go after the lost sheep until he finds it? And when he finds it, he joyfully puts it on his shoulders and goes home. Then he calls his friends and neighbors together and says, 'Rejoice with me; I have found my lost sheep.' I tell you that in the same way there will be more rejoicing in heaven over one sinner who repents than over ninety-nine righteous persons who do not need to repent.**" (Luke 15:3-7) This is comforting to those of us who struggle with always obeying God's command to "**be holy because I am holy.**" (1 Peter 1:16) Jesus loves sinners who repent. He delights is us whenever we confess our sins, more than the 99 'righteous' who do not. The reason for this is because confessing sinners are humble; for no man is "righteous" apart from the righteousness given to us by God's grace, through Jesus Christ his son. Many Christians struggle with their sins and overcoming them. It is a continual and exhausting wrestling match with our former fleshly desires. There is a way out of that dilemma. It is called 'walking in the Spirit.' **"This I say then, walk in the Spirit, and you shall not fulfil the lust of the flesh. For the flesh lusts against the Spirit, and the Spirit against the flesh: and these are contrary the one to the other: so that you cannot do the things that you would."**

(Galatians 5:16-17) So do not despair, God will do for us what we cannot do for ourselves, if we have a yielded and humble spirit. *"He guides me in the paths of righteousness for His name's sake."* (verse 3)

"Even though I walk through the valley of the shadow of death, I fear no evil, for You are with me." (verse 4) Death hangs over all humanity's heads like a guillotine. We never know when it is coming; but we know that someday it will strike us, and this life will end. We do whatever we can to avoid that day and to extend our lives. We try to avoid evil people and places and things that may harm us. Christians put their trust in Jesus to lead them. They are comforted because our Good Shepherd is always with us. *"Your rod and Your staff, they comfort me."* (verse 4) As "children of God," we are often referred to as, "God's flock of sheep." And just as a shepherd guides and protects his sheep, so does our Good Shepherd. When we stray, we may feel the hook of His *"staff"* about our

necks, pulling us back into His care. And when any dangerous threat or enemy seeks to devour us, He turns his staff about and uses his "***rod***" to beat away our enemies. Knowing this and placing our full confidence and faith in our Shepherd's love "***comforts***" us.

"***You prepare a table before me in the presence of my enemies; You have anointed my head with oil; my cup overflows.***" (verse 5) We all have enemies, either within or without us. No one gets away with avoiding trouble in life. We have been treated dishonorably, deceived, slandered, and robbed by our "***enemies.***" This is what God promises to do: He will "***prepare a table before me in the presence of my enemies.***" (verse 5) Whether in this life or in the next, they will see us lifted up above them, sitting with Christ and myriads of those who love Him. We will have inherited all the treasures of God. Our bodies will be glorious and eternal. The Bible says, "**The Son of Man will send out His angels, and they will weed out of His kingdom every cause of sin and all who practice lawlessness. And they will throw them into the fiery furnace, where there will be weeping and gnashing of teeth. Then the righteous will shine like the sun in the kingdom of their Father. He who has ears, let him hear.**" (Matthew 13:41-42)

"***You have anointed my head with oil; my cup overflows.***" (verse 5) Our anointing occurred when we received the Holy Spirit. Those who seek to walk in God's Spirit daily, express the love of God in their words and deeds. Just as Jesus, we are sent to give our lives in the service of God and to the world of mankind. This is the result and reward for those who do so, "**Give,**

and it will be given to you. A good measure, pressed down, shaken together, and running over, will be poured into your lap. For with the measure you use, it will be measured to you." (Luke 6:38)

Psalm 23 closes with a sweet verse that has great depth. "***Surely goodness and loving kindness will follow me all the days of my life, and I will dwell in the house of the LORD forever.***" (verse 6) Notice that it says, "***goodness and loving kindness will follow me.***" Inevitably, we will go through various trials, heartbreaks, and tribulation in this world, just as everyone does. But by faith we have learned that these times are an expression of our Lord's "***goodness and loving kindness.***" After the Lord strengthens our faith through trials, it is always followed by times of rest and refreshing. "**Consider it all joy, my brethren, when you encounter various trials, knowing that the testing of your faith produces endurance. And let endurance have its perfect result, so that you may be perfect and complete, lacking in nothing.**" (James 1:2-4) We learn through experience to rejoice in the Lord with true joy, despite anything we must endure in the world. Rain must fall for us to have "***green pastures***" and "***still waters.***" But through every experience we have in life, our Good Shepherd never leaves us; and for that we can always rejoice. David the King and Shepherd of Israel was a human with weaknesses, just like all of us. What he experienced with God is available to all. If we truly have faith and believe with all our heart that Jesus Christ is God's Holy Son, who gave His life so that we could live forever, and that our future is to live in the presence of the Lord in a beautiful city built just for us, then "***Surely goodness and loving kindness*** *will follow me all the days of my life, and I will dwell in the house of the LORD forever."*

Despite any trial we face, we always have reason to be glad in the Lord. He will come and deliver us. "**Sing praises to the Lord, O you his saints, and give thanks to his holy name. His anger is but for a moment, and his favor is for a lifetime. Weeping may tarry for the night, but joy comes with the morning.**" (Psalm 30:1-5)

Psalm 24

This psalm begins with a universal statement, confirming that there is one God. He made all that is seen and unseen, and he rules over them. "***The earth is the Lord's, and all it contains, the world, and those who dwell in it. For He has founded it upon the seas and established it upon the rivers.***" (verses 1-2) Unlike any celestial object that our astronomers discover, the Earth is the only one "***founded upon seas and established upon rivers***" of life-giving water. It is a unique and exclusive planet, chosen by the Creator for his fellowship and habitation with mankind. Now, David addresses the subject of his instruction: "***Who may ascend into the hill of the Lord? And who may stand in His holy place?***" (verse 3) The "***hill of the Lord***" refers to Mt. Zion, upon which the city of Jerusalem sits. It will be the home of Christ the King, and his faithful followers. This will occur on the refurbished earth that is to come, after the destruction of this edition of the earth. This total destruction is about to happen during the last 7 years on earth, the "Tribulation." That period of time is called "the Day of God's Wrath." His patience with the evil upon this earth will come to an end, just as in the days of Noah. The current city of Jerusalem will be replaced with a

New Jerusalem, which Christ has prepared for those who love him, and to dwell in with Him forever.

The prophets Ezekiel, Isaiah, and Zechariah gave precise details of the size and beauty of this city that shall come down from heaven. It shall be the capital of the world from where Christ will rule and maintain peace on earth. The Apostle John gives a description in his Book of Revelation: "**I did not see a temple in the city, because the Lord God Almighty and the Lamb are its temple. The city does not need the sun or the moon to shine on it, for the glory of God gives it light, and the Lamb is its lamp. The nations will walk by its light, and the kings of the earth will bring their splendor into it. On no day will its gates ever be shut, for there will be no night there. The glory and honor of the nations will be brought into it. Nothing impure will ever enter it, nor will anyone who does what is shameful or deceitful, but only those whose names are written in the Lamb's book of life.**" (Revelation 21:22-27)

Then, David describes the character of the people blessed and chosen to dwell with the Lord, "*He who has clean hands and a pure heart, who has not lifted up his soul to falsehood and has not sworn deceitfully.*" (verse 4) To have "clean hands" means that we do not involve ourselves with dirty deeds. To have a "*pure heart*" means that we do not allow our minds to even consider evil. For our God looks into the hearts of His people. He sees more than only our deeds. He sees our hearts' intent. In the Apostle Paul's wonderful description of Godly love, we are warned that if we do good but with a resentful heart, it accounts for nothing. "**If I speak in the tongues of** men or of angels, but do not have love, I am only a resounding gong or a clanging cymbal. If I have the gift of prophecy and can fathom all mysteries and all knowledge, and if I have a faith that can move mountains, but do not have love, I am nothing. If I give all I possess to the poor and give over my body to hardship that I may boast, but do not have love, I gain nothing." (1 Corinthians 13:1-3)

The good deeds we Christians do in being examples of Christ's love, are deeds stimulated by the love of God through the Holy Spirit living in our hearts. Therefore, we are told, "**Follow God's example, therefore, as dearly loved children and walk in the way of love, just as Christ loved us and gave himself up for us as a fragrant offering and sacrifice to God. But among you there must not be even a hint of sexual immorality, or of any kind of impurity, or of greed, because these are improper for God's holy people. Nor should there be obscenity, foolish talk, or coarse joking, which are out of place, but rather thanksgiving. For of this you can be sure: No immoral, impure, or greedy person—such a person is an idolater—has any inheritance in the kingdom of Christ and of God.**" (Ephesians 5:1- 5)

A person who has "***clean hands***" and a "***pure heart***" knows God intimately. The closer we get to His light the more darkness and evil intent is removed from us. A truly born-again Christian experiences a greater love, passion, and concern for others than they have ever known before. The "Agape" love of our righteous creator dwells in us and overcomes the sin. Consequently, we cannot take pride in the good that we do, for it is God's love that motivates and directs us to do these good things. "**For it is by grace you have been saved, through faith - and this not from yourselves, it is the gift of God - not by works, so that no one can boast. For we are God's workmanship, created in Christ Jesus to do good works, which God prepared in advance for us to do.**" (Ephesians 2:8-10)

The next part of this verse requires explanation and application. "*who does not trust in an idol or swear by a false god.*" (verse 4) Idolatry is not only the worship of images. Certainly, that was a major issue in the days of the Old Testament. There were idols and false Gods everywhere. God's chosen people were commanded to destroy all idols and false gods. "**Break down their altars and smash their sacred pillars. Burn their Asherah poles and cut down their carved idols. Completely erase the names of their gods!**" (Deuteronomy 12:3) However, God did not limit the definition of 'idols and false gods' to just images of religious worship and adoration. As we just read in Ephesians, "**No immoral, impure or greedy person—such a person is an idolater—has any inheritance in the kingdom of Christ and of God.**" (Ephesians 5:5) All sins are acts of idolatry. Immoral people worship the god of sex, thievery, lying, slander, anger, money, politics, oppression, bigotry, … They are "**greedy**" because they serve themselves and material things as god. They have fleshly, selfish desires and passions that are satisfied without any concern for the damage caused to others. This is human nature. That is why Jesus said that we "must be born again," not by the flesh but of the Spirit of God's holiness.

Jesus was asked, "**Teacher, which commandment is the greatest in the Law?**" Jesus declared, "**Love the Lord your God with all your heart and with all your soul and with all your mind. This is the first and greatest commandment. And the second is like it: 'Love your neighbor as yourself.**" (Matthew 22:37-38) If Jehovah is truly our God, then we are obliged to seek Him, and to revere and to honor Him above all people and things. Our hearts' primary desire is always to please God by doing what he asks: Love Him and others. Seek to serve humanity as our Lord Jesus demonstrated. Put the needs of others before our own. As the apostle Paul so eloquently said, "**Do nothing out of selfish ambition or empty pride, but in humility consider others more important than yourselves. Each of you should look not only to your own interests but also to the interest of others. Let this mind be in you which was also in Christ Jesus.**" (Philippians 2:4)

It is this understanding that readies us for the next verse of Psalm 24, "*He shall receive a blessing from the Lord and righteousness from the God of his salvation. This is the generation of those who seek Him, who seek Your face—even Jacob. Selah.*" (verses 5-6) Living for God, instead of for ourselves, has great rewards. The first blessing we receive when we turn away from serving ourselves and repent of our sins is "*righteousness.*" When any sinner confesses his immoralities, impurities and greed to Jesus Christ, their sins are forgiven and forgotten. "**If we confess our sins, he is faithful and just and will forgive us our sins and purify us from all unrighteousness.**" (1 John 1:9) We are "**purified**" by the Holy Spirit, day by day, as we die to ourselves and live for others. But first we are made righteous as a gift from our Savior.

The Great News of the message of Christ is: Simply by believing in Him we are saved from death and receive the gift of eternal life in the paradise of God! This is the same way that all people have received forgiveness, righteousness, and salvation. Just as Father Abraham was saved, we are too, "**And he believed the Lord, and he counted it to him as righteousness.**" (Genesis 15:6)

The closing verses of Psalm 24 are particularly beautiful. Once again, David the seer and prophet, shares the vision God has given to all of the prophets, apostles and believers in Christ concerning His triumphant return. "*Lift up your heads, oh gates, and be lifted up, oh ancient doors, that the King of glory may come in! Who is the King of glory? The Lord strong and mighty, the Lord mighty in battle. Lift up your heads, oh gates, and lift them up, Oh ancient doors, that the King of glory may come in! Who is this King of glory? The Lord of hosts, He is the King of glory. Selah.*" (verses 7-10) These "*gates*" and "*doors*" refer to one of the various entrance ways into the ancient city. The oldest of the current gates in Jerusalem's Old City Walls is the Golden Gate. It is prophesied that Christ will enter through this eastern Gate, when He, the "Anointed One (King Jesus)" comes. Indeed, this is the gate whereby Jesus entered the Temple area the day before his crucifixion, when the people shouted, "**Hosanna! to the Son of David! Blessed is he who comes in the name of the Lord!" Hosanna in the highest heaven!**" (Matthew 21:9)

Here is Ezekiel's vision of Jesus coming through the Golden Gate when He returns to rule, **"Then the man (angel) brought me to the gate facing east, and I saw the glory of the God of Israel coming from the east. His voice was like the roar of rushing waters, and the land was radiant with his glory. I fell facedown. The glory of the Lord entered the temple through the gate facing east. Then the Spirit lifted me up and brought me into the inner court, and the glory of the Lord filled the temple ... While the man (angel) was standing beside me, I heard someone speaking to me from inside the temple. He said: "Son of man, this is the place of my throne and the place for the soles of my feet. This is where I will live among the Israelites forever."** (Ezekiel 43:1-7) Psalm 24 instructs us in the ways of salvation and righteousness. Then it closes with the wonderful promise of Christ's triumphal return to bring peace to the world. That day is near. It is essential that we all examine ourselves and ask, "Am I ready for the coming of the '***King of Glory***?" (verse 10)

Psalm 25

Not to revere God is foolishness. God adores those who adore Him. They are the "humble" of the world. It is with this understanding and knowledge that David calls upon the Lord. "*To You, O Lord, I lift up my soul. O my God, in You I trust, do not let me be ashamed; do not let my enemies exult over me. Indeed, none of those who wait for You will be ashamed; those who deal treacherously without cause will be ashamed.*" (verses 1-3)

God loves the humble. It begins with fearing God. "**The fear of the Lord is the beginning of wisdom; a good understanding have all those who do His commandments; His praise endures forever.**" (Psalm 111:10) If we fear anything, we should fear the Lord. Why? Because He is the One who decides our destiny, and who will judge us when our body dies. He determines where we will reside for eternity, with Him in Glory, or "**cast into outer darkness, where there will be weeping and the gnashing of teeth.**" (Matt. 22:13-14)

The wise trust in God. To Him alone do they "*lift up*" their souls. If we are known to be believers in Christ, a people who trusts in God and who obeys His Law of Love, then we never want to do or say anything that will bring shame to ourselves. By so doing, we also bring shame upon other believers who confess their faith publicly. Impatience with God, the lack of our trust and confidence in Him, will lead us to disgraceful behavior. But those whose faith causes them to patiently wait: "***Indeed, none of those who wait for You will be ashamed.***" (verse 3a) Whereas those who fail to trust the Lord and turn to other means and ways will fall into disgrace: "***those who deal treacherously without cause will be ashamed.***" (verse 3b)

Waiting for the Lord to respond and answer our desperate prayers is one of the hardest things for us to do. It is like having a horrible toothache and having to wait a few days before the dentist can see you. It can seem unbearable when we pray, and he does not answer right away. Of course, the Lord has heard our prayers, but he permits us for good purposes to wait for a time, occasionally. Once again, our primary purpose in life is to develop a confident faith in God's immense love for us. Finding peace in the midst of toil, trouble and heartbreak is a fruit of the Spirit. Many can bear up under physical and emotional anguish. But waiting for the Lord to respond to our prayers can be more difficult. Waiting builds our faith and confidence in God.

David had gone through many dangers and trials that seemed impossible from which to escape. His faith was hardened by experience. David knew for certainty that God was his friend; therefore, he can state, "***Indeed, none of those who wait for You will be ashamed.***" (verse 3a)

True and faithful followers of the Lord God are implanted with this desire within their hearts: "***Make me know Your ways,***

O Lord; teach me Your paths. Lead me in Your truth and teach me, for You are the God of my salvation; for You I wait all the day." (verses 4-5) They are eager to be wise and knowledgeable in the ways of their Maker and Master. They believe in His word. They know Jehovah offers them eternal salvation through the sacrifice and resurrection of the Lamb of God, Jesus Christ. Even when our prayers are not answered as we wished, we praise Him for that too; for, we are always confident in God's righteousness, wisdom, and love. If we die, then we go to the Lord. If we suffer, we rejoice because we are permitted to share in the sufferings of our Savior. The loss or lack of worldly goods does not concern us. We persevere. We endure. The faith that God gave us when we believed grows stronger when we are persecuted for righteousness sake. We declare that others can have all the things of this world. We will seek for the things concerning the Kingdom of God: love, righteousness, joy, and peace. *"Remember, O Lord, your compassion and your loving kindnesses, for they have been from of old. Do not remember the sins of my youth or my transgressions; according to Your lovingkindness remember me, for Your goodness' sake, O Lord."* (verses 6-7) Certainly, we have all fallen short of being perfect. Hopefully, as we have grown in the Spirit of the Lord, the sins of our youth and its iniquities have been largely defeated. If we have confessed these sins and asked for the Lord's forgiveness, then be assured that he has erased all of those sins. They are no longer on His record books. However, although the Lord has forgotten them, He does not want us to do so. They are reminders of where we were and where God has taken us since. They are reasons for daily rejoicing. Those memories may come to mind and strike us in our heart's conscience occasionally. They make us feel remorseful. They humble us and are reminders of our Great Shepherd's love and power to transform us. These moments are always followed by words of praise and thanksgiving to our Redeemer and Savior. They remind us of our unworthiness and make us fall to our knees in gratitude for God's amazing grace!

"He leads the humble in justice, and He teaches the humble His way. All the paths of the Lord are lovingkindness and truth to those who keep His covenant and His testimonies." (verses 9-10) Humility is essential for a successful Christian life. We cannot walk in the Spirit without it. If we are not humble, then we are proud: either one or the other. "**All of you, clothe yourselves with humility toward one another, for God is opposed to the proud, but gives grace to the humble. Therefore, humble yourselves under the mighty hand of God, that He may exalt you at the proper time, casting all your anxiety on Him, because He cares for you... After you have suffered for a little while, the God of all grace, who called you to His eternal glory in Christ, will Himself perfect, confirm, strengthen and establish you.**" (1 Peter 5:5-7,10)Christians often have the attitude that our life right now is a testing ground. Just as soldiers must complete "Boot Camp" before becoming officially a member of the US Military, we must pass our life's tests to prove that we are truly committed and ready to serve God faithfully forever. We are convinced that our real life comes afterward. Therefore, when we pass through fire and flood, we are not scorched nor drowned. We endure, persevere, and do so in faith, with rejoicing, know-

ing that it is God shaping us into His image. We are thankful because we long to be like Jesus. We earnestly desire to please God in all things. That is our greatest joy! "**Consider it all joy, my brethren, when you encounter various trials, knowing that the testing of your faith produces endurance. And let endurance have its perfect result, so that you may be perfect and complete, lacking in nothing.**" (James 1:2-4)

"*For Your name's sake, O Lord, pardon my iniquity, for it is great.*" (verse 11) What does it mean, "*for your name's sake*"? We read this phrase often throughout the Bible. There is only one true God. He is a God of love, mercy, compassion, and forgiveness. That is the true meaning of his Name. This is why Christians believe, behave, praise, pray, and share the gospel, "*for His name's sake.*"

These are some of the promises with which our Maker swears to fulfill for all who trust in Him: "*Who is the man who fears the Lord? He will instruct him in the way he should choose. His soul will abide in prosperity, and his descendants will inherit the land. the secret of the Lord is for those who fear Him, and He will make them know His covenant. My eyes are continually toward the Lord, for He will pluck my feet out of the net.*" (verses 12-15)

David pleads once again for God to help him and to guard his soul. "*Bring me out of my distresses. Look upon my affliction and my trouble and forgive all my sins. Look upon my enemies, for they are many, and they hate me with violent hatred. Guard my soul and deliver me; do not let me be ashamed, for I take refuge in You. Let integrity and uprightness preserve me, for I wait for You.*" (verses 17-21) He pleas for Jehovah to preserve him in "***integrity and uprightness.***" And until God performs these requests, David promises to "***wait***." When we wait patiently and without complaint for our Deliver to come, it is proof of our faith. It is in the process of waiting that faith grows stronger, and by which God often answers our prayers.

"***Redeem Israel, oh God, out of all his troubles.***" (verse 22) As in many of his psalms, David closes with a prayer for his people, Israel. This is in harmony with this psalm. God calls all of followers to love and to serve eachother. We are commanded to pray for eachother too. "***Therefore, confess your sins to each other and pray for each other so that you may be healed. The prayer of a righteous man is powerful and effective.***" (James 5:16)

Psalm 26

"*Vindicate me, O Lord, for I have walked in my integrity, and I have trusted in the Lord without wavering. Examine me, O Lord, and try me; test my mind and my heart. For Your lovingkindness is before my eyes, and I have walked in Your truth.*" (verses 1-3) The definition of "***vindicate***" is to 'acquit, clear, absolve, exonerate." This what the Lord offers all who trust in Him. David professes that he has "***trusted in the Lord without wavering,***" (verse 1) and that he has "***walked in Your truth.***" (verse 3b) David had given his whole heart to seek God and His righteousness. He knew the greatest truth in the cosmos: God rewards those that walk in His ways. Therefore, David asks to be "***examined***;" even for God to "***test***" his confidence in God's love.

David has not been ignorant of his Lord's continual blessing: "***For Your lovingkindness is before my eyes.***" This is critical to being a godly believer. Let us ask the Lord to open our eyes and for us to become aware of and to see His myriads of blessing showered upon us every day. But the greatest blessing is yet to be fulfilled. Someday we will see Christ our Lord face to face in His majesty and power. Christians will be embraced by Him. Literally, God will hold us in his loving arms. He will give each of us a private and special name, known only to us and Him. And we will live on a new earth, recreated for us in perfection and splendor. David then prays for God to give him discernment to know who among his congregation are *"pretenders who are deceitful."* David refuses to have fellowship with them, just as we are exhorted to do in the New Testament. **"Don't team up with those who are unbelievers. How can righteousness be a partner with wickedness? How can light live with darkness? What harmony can there be between Christ and the devil? How can a believer be a partner with an unbeliever? And what union can there be between God's temple and idols? For we are the temple of the living God. As God said: "I will live in them and walk among them. I will be their God, and they will be my people. therefore, come out from among unbelievers, and separate yourselves from them, says the Lord, don't touch their filthy things, and I will welcome you."** (2 Corinthians 6:14-17)

In addition to walking in love and in righteousness, God also asks us to be thankful and to praise Him continually. He requests this for our good. The more that we open our hearts, minds, eyes, and ears to see all that He has done for us throughout our lives, we are humbled by his love, and praise is the natural result. We have all received from the Lord's hands what we do not deserve. *"I will go about Your altar, O Lord, that I may proclaim with the voice of thanksgiving and declare all Your wonders."* (verses 6b-7)

In every book of the Bible true believers are exhorted to gather together, *"O Lord, I love the habitation of Your house and the place where Your glory dwells."* (verse 8) God's glory resides within His church, the body of Christ. Nowhere on earth is there a better place to be than among Christians who worship and thank our Lord for His infinite works, and for the promise of our heavenly inheritance. Therefore, Jesus tells us, **"For where two or three gather in my name, there am I with them."** (Matthew 18:20)

David then closes with the point of his petition, *"Do not take my soul away along with sinners ...for I shall walk in my integrity; redeem me and be gracious to me."* (verse 11) David then makes a statement of gratitude, *"My foot stands on a level place."* (verse 12) This reminds us of Jesus' parable about two men: a fool and a wise man. One built his house on sand, which is unstable and shifts with the wind. The other built his house on a rock, which is solid and stable. **"Therefore, everyone who hears these words of mine and puts them into practice is like a wise man who built his house on the rock. The rain came down, the streams rose, and the winds blew and beat against that house; yet it did not fall, because it had its foundation on the rock. But everyone who hears these words of mine and does not put them into practice is like a foolish man who built his house on sand. The rain came down, the streams rose, and the winds blew and beat against that house, and it fell with a great crash."** (Matthew 7:24-27) In this last line, David makes a declaration and a promise: *"In the congregations I shall bless the Lord."* (verse 12b) David will not keep silent about the goodness he receives from God. He will declare it to the people. He will publicly *"bless the Lord."* In church, and out, we are to be thankful for God's grace and to testify to others about his love.

Psalm 27

What a wonderful blessing to have our God and Maker personally lead, provide, and defend us throughout our lives. "***The Lord is my light and my salvation.***" (verse 1) Those who have been healed by God's grace from addiction, immorality, and afflictions know what darkness is. It is when all hope is lost. Perhaps we have all felt this way sometimes. Many years ago, I became extremely depressed. I was handicapped and struggling to support my young wife and child. Life had not turned out like I had imagined it would. We were poor and always full of anxiety about tomorrow. My wife and I saw no way out. We felt like were in an endlessly long, dark tunnel from which we would never escape. One night, we prayed to the Lord something like this: "Lord we are in complete darkness. We see no way out of our troubles. We do not know what to do. Please lead us into your Light. Help us, Lord!" -- Just by taking our burdens in contrite humility and giving them to our Holy Shepherd, we felt better. Slowly, from that day, things began to improve. Within a few years, we owned a 3-bedroom house at the beach and were not concerned about how much we had in the bank. Life was easy for a while. Then, unforeseen difficulties beyond our control wiped out all of our savings. Soon, we were poorer than ever! But this time we were not terrified nor dismayed. The Lord had taken us out of poverty before, and we were confident that He would again. So, like David we could say, "**Whom shall I fear? The Lord is the defense of my life. Whom shall I dread?**" (verse 1b) Since then, we have had many ups and downs. We have grown old enough to know this is true for almost everyone. The most painful experiences are when those we love and trust betray us. Despite all of our goodness that we shower upon them, they turn on us and seek our destruction. Deception and unrequited love are difficult to endure. Certainly, it breaks our hearts. But this happens in life. It destroys some people and makes others bitter. Yet, if we know for certain that Jesus is our defender, provider, and Good Shepherd, then we can declare this in peace. "**When evildoers came upon me to devour my flesh, my adversaries and my enemies, they stumbled and fell. Though a host encamp against me, my heart will not fear; though war arise against me, in spite of this I shall be confident.**" (verses 2-3) This is possible because we have been born-again spiritually and have received the gift of faith by the Holy Spirit. In spite of whatever comes against us we "**shall be confident.**"

As we grow in the Lord and bear His godly fruit in our lives, our hearts are transformed. We fall in love with God. More than anything or person or pleasure, walking in a manner that pleases Jesus becomes our hearts' greatest desire. Those who walk in loving fellowship with the Lord, fully understand what Jesus declared, **"Anyone who loves their father or mother more than me is not worthy of me; anyone who loves their** son or daughter more than me is not worthy of me." (Matthew 10:37) We grow to understand our complete dependence on God. He is our life, breath, health, provider, and defender. God is love. No one loves us more. Those who love God, also seek Him every day. Thus, David writes, "**One thing I have asked from the Lord, that I shall seek: That I may dwell in the house of the Lord all the days of my life, to behold the beauty of the Lord and to meditate in His temple.**" (verse 4)

David sometime refers to Jehovah as his "**hiding place.**" Where is this refuge? It is whenever and wherever we trust in God with all our heart and soul. That is why Christians worship and rejoice in song and praise. God gives us hope, confidence and strength. He makes us to stand upon solid ground. Despite the plots of our enemies, our Lord leads us to safety "**For in the day of trouble He will conceal me in His tabernacle. In the secret place of His tent He will hide me. He will lift me up on a rock. And now my head will be lifted up above my enemies around me, and I will offer in His tent sacrifices with shouts of joy; I will sing, yes, I will sing praises to the Lord.**" (verses 5-6)

David sought to walk in the paths of righteousness that God gave to Moses, with all of his mind, heart, strength, and soul. "**Hear, O Lord, when I cry with my voice, and be gracious to me and answer me. When You said, "Seek My face," my heart said to You, "Your face, O Lord, I shall seek." Do not hide Your face from me, do not turn Your servant away in anger.**" (verses 7-9) Children of God earnestly desire to please our Lord in all things. We know that our Father will correct and discipline us if we ignore his commands and drift away from following Him. David knows that the Lord hears him, and that God will reply because he has submitted to the Lord as the Master of his life. That is the source of David's joy!

Now, David says something entirely personal that many of us may experience too. *"**For my father and my mother have forsaken me, but the Lord will take me up.**"* (verse 10) Some of us may not have had loving and caring parents. This makes it more difficult to trust others, especially God. David may have experienced this too. In chapter 16 of the first book of Samuel David, as a young boy, is chosen by God to someday replace Saul as King in Judah and Israel. The Lord had told the prophet to go to the home of Jesse, David's father, and to anoint the son that God chooses. Jesse brought seven sons before Samuel. **"The Lord has not chosen these."** So, he asked Jesse, **"Are these all the sons you have? "There is still the youngest," Jesse answered. "He is tending the sheep."** (1 Samuel 16:10-11) Unlike his impressive, tall brothers who were soldiers in Saul's army, David was a boy shepherd. He did not sleep at home much because sheep need constant tending. He seems to have been the "runt" of the litter, and not embraced with the love of his family. His own father had to be asked, **"Are these all the sons you have?"** Later, when David goes to give food to his brothers, who are with Saul and facing off against the Philistines and Goliath, his brothers are rude and insulting to him too. Some of us may have grown up unloved and can say this along with David, *"**my father and my mother have forsaken me.**"* (verse 10) But our wonderful God loves the unloved, the rejected, the abused, the oppressed, the afflicted, and the broken hearted. They are special to Him. Therefore, Jesus says,

"Come to Me, all who are weary and heavy-laden, and I will give you rest. "Take My yoke upon you and learn from Me, for I am gentle and humble in heart, and you will find rest for your souls. For My yoke is easy and My burden is light." (Matthew 11: 28-30)Jehovah loves us more than we will ever comprehend, certainly far more than any human is possible of loving us. That is why He is more important to us than anything or anyone on earth, and for whom we will gladly give our lives. We live to please Him rather than ourselves. Therefore, with David, Christians pray this, "***Teach me Your way, O Lord, and lead me in a level path…***" (verse 11a)

The next part of this verse relates this to David's specific situation, "***because of my foes.***" (verse 11b) Our "***foes***" are the enemies that persecute us. These foes may cause us to stray from our Lord's path of righteousness. The anxiety and stress they cause us can make us seek relief by finding temporary pleasure in sin. To avoid this, in David's times of worry and grief he turns to our God and pleads, as we do too, "***Teach me Your way, O Lord, and lead me in a level path because of my foes.***" (verse 11)

"***Wait for the Lord. Be strong and let your heart take courage. Yes, wait for the Lord.***" (verse 14) This one verse has been the bulwark of my life and my walk with God. The Holy Spirit had me read this when our business was wiped out. That day was a major blow, becoming penniless in one day! At first, we were terrified. And then the Spirit had me read this verse. "**God is faithful. He will not allow the temptation to be more than you can stand. When you are tempted, he will show you a**

way out so that you can endure." (1 Corinthians 10:13) Like David, I also encourage all Believers to be strong and courageous. When all else fails our Good Shepherd is still with us. Wait for Him. He will show you a way out after he has accomplished his fatherly purposes. When we chose to take our first step toward God by believing that He loves us so much that He became man and died in man's place to pay the penalty of our sins, God instills within us a faith that is not our own. It is by the gift of His strength that we stand firm! "**For by grace are you saved through faith; and that is not of yourselves; it is the gift of God.**" (Ephesians 2:8)

Psalm 28

David begins this psalm like many others. He states that without God being present in his life that he is totally lost. David makes his supplication by declaring to the Lord that without His help he would be in deep despair. *"To You, O Lord, I call; my rock, do not be deaf to me; for, if You are silent to me, I will become like those who go down to the pit. Hear the voice of my supplications when I cry to You for help, when I lift up my hands toward Your holy sanctuary."* (verses 1-2) It is vital that when we come before our Creator that we do so in complete humility and reverence for Him. So, David declares his dependence on Jehovah and cries out for His immediate assistance. He lifts his hands as he does so. This is a posture of contrition, humility, and the means of honoring the Lord as he makes his request.

"Do not drag me away with the wicked and with those who work iniquity, who speak peace with their neighbors, while evil is in their hearts." (verse 3) David knows the end of all who turn away from God and who practice doing what the Lord forbids. People who seek the Lord and his righteousness will always attract those who seek to take an advantage of us

because of our universal love for humanity and our earnest concern for all people. They are the pretenders of whom Jesus says, "**They come to you in sheep's clothing, but inwardly they are ferocious wolves.**" (Matthew 7:15)

Christians are instructed to be lights in the world and to shine forth the love of God. We are also told to be wary and wise and not to let wolves into our fellowship. But it can be hard to always discover them because they are disguised as sheep. Therefore, David asks the Lord, who knows every intent of our hearts to find them out and to judge them appropriately. "*Repay them according to their work and according to the evil of their practices. Requite them according to the deeds of their hands. Repay them their recompense. Because they do not regard the works of the Lord nor the deeds of His hands, He will tear them down and not build them up.*" (verses 4-5)

Again, we must never forget to live our lives in the fear of the Lord, unless we fall away and "*do not regard the works of the Lord nor the deeds of His hands.*" For, those who become lazy in their faith and do not seek after the Lord, along with the wicked "*He will tear them down and not build them up.*"- David now praises the Lord, "*Blessed be the Lord, because He has heard the voice of my supplication.*" (verse 6) This is also how we should pray. Always come before God with praise and in humility, knowing that He made us and not we ourselves. Truly, consider how wonderful it is to be certain that the God of the universe hears us when we speak to Him in this way.

"*The Lord is my strength and my shield. My heart trusts in Him, and I am helped; therefore, my heart exults, and*

with my song I shall thank Him." (verse 7) David exalts in the Lord and thanks Him for giving him the strength to endure the onslaughts of evil men and the hardships of life. David takes time to meditate on God's words and then to compose songs to Him. Without dispute, the more time we spend reading the Bible slowly, and meditating and praying as we do, the more we will trust in the Lord.

"The Lord is their strength, and He is a saving defense to His anointed. Save Your people and bless Your inheritance; be their shepherd also and carry them forever." (verses 8-9) Not only as king, but as a fellow believer and as a shepherd to Judah and Israel, David asks for the blessings of God to be also given to his people. This is critical for all believers to practice when praying. The key to living a life that is always bearing the holy fruit of God's Spirit is to die to living for ourselves, and to live to please God. This always results in a far greater love for humanity. God's intent for the lives of his children is for them to be bright lights set on a hill in a dark world. The more that we surrender to God's Holy Spirit within us and die to our fleshly desires, the brighter our light becomes; and the more loving, compassionate, and gentle we become. It is by God's love manifesting itself in our lives that attracts people to us, and which opens their hearts and minds to receive our message from the world's only God and Savior.

Psalm 29

King David begins this psalm with an exhortation to consider who the Lord is that we serve and worship. This is important for us each to do each day and throughout the day. Since we live in fleshly, mortal bodies whose cravings for sinful pleasures never cease, it is vital that believers begin everyday by taking time with our eternal God in order to stimulate His Spirit within us. *"Attribute to the Lord, O sons of the mighty, attribute to the Lord glory and strength. Attribute to the Lord the glory due to His name; worship the Lord in holy array."* (verse 12) David addresses his audience as *"O sons of the mighty."* He is specifically referring to believers. How fortunate we are to be called *"sons."* By this word God means all those who call upon his name, male or female. **"So, in Christ Jesus you are all children of God through faith in Christ Jesus."** (Galatians 3:26)

This psalm focuses on the glorious strength and power of God. He rules over all the natural forces of Nature. *"He makes Lebanon skip like a calf, and Sirion like a young wild ox. The voice of the Lord hews out flames of fire. The voice of the Lord shakes the wilderness; the Lord shakes the wilderness of Kadesh.*" (verses 6-8) These verses may be referring to major earthquakes that happened in the Middle East during David's reign and afterward. Cities were leveled, mountains collapsed, floods occurred, fires erupted… It must have seemed like the end of the world. Whether they understood that this is a natural event caused from the shifting of the earth's crust or not, David declares to his people that God is in charge of all events that happen on earth. He rules over Nature. "***The voice of the Lord is powerful. The voice of the Lord is majestic.***" (verse 4)

As we approach the end of this age of the earth, and the beginning of Christ's rule upon the earth, we are beginning to see what Jesus predicted. "**As Jesus was sitting on the Mount of Olives, the disciples came to him privately. "Tell us," they said, "when will this happen, and what will be the sign of your coming and of the end of the age? …There will be famines and earthquakes in various places. All these are the beginning of birth pains.**" (Matthew 24:3-9)

Famines are happening. Islands are being engulfed by the ocean. Our polar ice is melting at an alarming rate. The Sahara Desert is expanding and destroying the ability of people to survive in sub-Saharan countries. The Amazon Rain Forest, the "lungs of the earth," are being burned and destroyed. Famines and deadly viruses are creating mass migrations of people and putting stress upon other nations of the world. As a consequence, nations are closing the borders and becoming nationalistic and "xenophobic" (fear and hatred of strangers or foreigners.) The love of mankind is growing colder as our earth gets hotter. This will lead to global wars, which will culminate at the battle of Armageddon outside of Jerusalem. That is the appointed time for Christ to descend from heaven, destroy those armies, and to begin his reign as King of Righteousness over the world. That is the moment that Enoch prophesied about when he said: "**Behold, the Lord comes with ten thousands of His saints, to execute judgment on all, to convict all who are ungodly among them of all their ungodly deeds which they have committed in an ungodly way, and of all the harsh things which ungodly sinners have spoken against Him.**" (Jude, verses 14-15).

Christ is coming with all who have believed in him with an enduring faith. They are his "bride," his "church." These believers will be taken out of this world prior to the 7 last years of its fall and destruction. God will do so because the final 7 years on earth are for his judgement and wrath to be poured out upon an unbelieving world. Many millions will repent and turn to God during this time. But those of us who believed before the time of "great tribulation," this is promised, "**It will happen in a moment, in the blink of an eye, when the last trumpet is blown. For when the trumpet sounds, those who have died will be raised to live forever. And we who are living will also be transformed. For our dying bodies must be transformed into bodies that will never die; our mortal bodies must be transformed into immortal bodies… So, my dear brothers and sisters, be strong and immovable. Always work enthusiastically for the Lord, for you know that nothing you do for the Lord is ever useless.**" (1 Corinthians 15:51-58)

David now concludes his psalm with two reminders: God is the ruler over all Nature, including the flood that once destroyed us, and the fiery destruction to come. But we who trust in Him can have peace in the midst of this world's strife. "***The Lord sat as King at the flood. Yes, the Lord sits as King forever. The Lord will give strength to His people. The Lord will bless His people with peace.***" (verse 10-11)

David was a major prophet. The revelations given to him about Jesus Christ, and his death and resurrection, are incontrovertible proof of David being given extraordinary foresight into the future. In this psalm he boasts of the Lord's strength as shown in storms and upheavals in Nature. Then in later psalms and by prophets who came afterwards, the Holy Scriptures refer to the world ending again. The purpose of this psalm of David's is to tell us how to be protected from God's fury, "***Ascribe to the Lord, you heavenly beings, ascribe to the Lord glory and strength. Ascribe to the Lord the glory due his name; worship the Lord in the splendor of his holiness.***" (verse 2)

Psalm 30

These are the words of every person who has realized their sinfulness and turned to God. "*I will extol You, O Lord, for You have lifted me up, and have not let my enemies rejoice over me. O Lord my God, I cried to You for help, and You healed me.*" (verses 1-2) This is the testimony of all who have received Jesus with a sincere and open heart. We are acutely aware of our sinful past, and amazed and extremely grateful that God rescued us from our fast track to Hell; and kept us alive long enough to be enlightened, to repent, and to seek God earnestly in praise and adoration for his overwhelming love and kindness toward us who believe. "*O Lord, you have brought up my soul from Sheol. You have kept me alive, so that I would not go down to the pit.*" (verse 3) This is the reason for the next verse, "*Sing praise to the Lord, you His godly ones, and give thanks to His holy name.*" (verse 4)

Throughout the entire Bible, God calls to us and encourages us to come to Him and be saved from our enemies. In Isaiah, He says, "**Then your light will break forth like the dawn, and your healing will quickly appear; then 'your Righteous One' will go before you, and the glory of the Lord will be your**

rear guard." (Isaiah 58:8) Our "**Righteous One**" is Jesus. He goes before us and behind us. He encompasses us round about. As we follow Him, putting our feet where He walks, Christ leads us into the Light and heals us of our iniquities and afflictions. David has experienced God's anger, as we who belong to Him do when we go astray. Life becomes much more difficult. But David has repented and asked God to heal him from his sinful ways and from the damage it has done to his life and reputation. David is assured that God, in His lovingkindness, will forgive him and restore him. "*For His anger is but for a moment; yet His favor is for a lifetime.*" (verse 5) Therefore, David thanks the Lord for forgiving him and restoring his strength, so that he could overcome his enemies. "*O Lord, by your favor you have made my mountain stand strong.*" (verse 7)

We all sin. We are always at war between the desires of our flesh and the desires of God's Spirit within us. No one can achieve victory over our adversaries without the power of God on our side. The power to defeat our sinful desires is beyond mere human will power. Only God can heal us. Fortunately, our Maker is full of grace, love, and kindness. He knows our weaknesses and He is always ready to forgive us when we sincerely confess and turn away from our sin. "*Weeping may last for the night, but a shout of joy comes in the morning.*" (verse 5)

Now we get an insight into what David did to cause God's anger toward him. "*Now as for me, I said in my prosperity, "I will never be moved."*" (verse 6) This is pride. It is a sin that tempts rulers. It was the reason for the seven years of madness imposed upon King Nebuchadnezzar of Babylon, "**You will** be driven away from people and will live with the wild animals; you will eat grass like the ox and be drenched with the dew of heaven. Seven times will pass by for you until you acknowledge that the Most High is sovereign over all kingdoms on earth and gives them to anyone he wishes." (Daniel 4:25)

We are reminded to never be proud of ourselves and our accomplishments. **"It is because of Him that you are in Christ Jesus, who has become for us wisdom from God: our righteousness, holiness, and redemption. Therefore, as it is written: "Let him who boasts boast in the Lord."** (1 Corinthians 1:31) Jeremiah says it like this, **"This is what the LORD says: "Let not the wise man boast in his wisdom, nor the strong man in his strength, nor the wealthy man in his riches. But let him who boasts boast in this, that he understands and knows Me, that I am the LORD, who exercises loving devotion, justice and righteousness on the earth; for I delight in these things," declares the LORD."** (Jeremiah 9:24)

David has confessed and repented of his prideful thoughts. He has been humbled by the Lord and made to remember that it is by God's grace alone that he and all of us are blessed with what we have. *"O Lord, by Your favor You have made my mountain to stand strong. You hid Your face, I was dismayed. To You, O Lord, I called, and to the Lord I made supplication: "What profit is there in my blood, if I go down to the pit? Will the dust praise You? Will it declare Your faithfulness? "Hear, O Lord, and be gracious to me. O Lord, be my helper."* (verses 7-10) David pleads for the Lord to forgive him. He declares that it is the Lord who has made him a mighty ruler, not himself. He begs the Lord to spare his life so that he can continue to praise God and declare his marvelous deeds.

This is all that the Lord asks of us, to serve Him and not ourselves; and to understand that all that we have is from His hands of mercy. These are the prayers of contrition that He desires. By so doing, we receive this, "*You have turned for me my mourning into dancing; You have loosed my sackcloth and girded me with gladness, that my soul may sing praise to You and not be silent. O Lord my God, I will give thanks to You forever.*" (verses 11-12)

Psalm 31

David is obviously in great peril when he writes this. All rulers are targets for envious and self-seeking people. There are always those that seek to dethrone a leader. Leaders are in a position to be criticized and hated. But we non-leaders also experience persecution and hatred because of our faith. Our beliefs set us apart from the masses of unbelievers. It also makes us targets. Hence, David cries out to our God, "*In you, Lord, I have taken refuge; let me never be put to shame. Deliver me in your righteousness.* (verse 1)God is completely holy. He is Truth and He is Life. The universe and all the laws God has set in place to preserve it are dependent on God's absolute perfection. Otherwise, the order of the micro and macro cosmos would become chaos and destroy itself. No human can possibly attain to the perfection that God and His Christ possess, unless God grants His perfect righteousness to us as a gift. This is the Good News of the message of Jesus Christ.

David does not insist that God *deliver* Him because of David's own righteousness. The Bible teaches us that "**None is righteous, no, not one; no one understands; no one seeks for God. All have turned aside; together they have become**

worthless; no one does good, not even one." (Romans 3:11-12) Therefore, David, as we should do too, does not come before the Maker of the worlds declaring that he deserves God's help because of his goodness. No. David makes his plea on the basis of God's righteousness. "*In Your righteousness deliver me. Turn your ear to me, come quickly to my rescue; be my rock of refuge, a strong fortress to save me. Since You are my rock and my fortress, for the sake of your name lead and guide me. Keep me free from the trap that is set for me, for you are my refuge.*" (verses 1-4) David often had to escape to caves in the rocks of the wilderness for refuge and to hide from Saul and his assassins. But David did not trust in caves to protect himself. No. David put his trust in the Lord of heaven and earth, the one and only savior. Therefore, David professes his confidence and faith in God, and claims, "*You are my rock and my fortress.*" (verse 2)

Jesus himself is referred to in the bible as a 'rock of living water' and as a 'stone' of stumbling. "**And did all drink the same spiritual drink: for they drank of a spiritual rock that followed them: and the rock was Christ.**" (1 Corinthians 10:4) And, "**To you who believe, then, this stone is precious. But to those who do not believe, "The stone the builders rejected has become the cornerstone**, and, "**A stone of stumbling and a rock of offense.**" **They stumble because they disobey the message—and to this they were appointed.**" (1 Peter 2:8)

This could be the daily prayer for the entire Christian church. "*Into your hands I commit my spirit; deliver me, Lord, my faithful God. I abhor those who cling to worthless idols; as for me, I trust in the Lord. I will be glad and rejoice in your love, for you saw my affliction and knew the anguish of my soul. You have not given me into the hands of the enemy but have set my feet in a spacious place."* (verses 5-9) These are words that every Christian can say with deepest sincerity and with fullness of heart because they are true for all followers of Christ, who is the Messiah, the King of Kings and Lord of Lords, God's Holy Son, our Redeemer, Ransom, and Reward.

John the apostle explained, **"God is spirit, and those who worship Him must worship in spirit and truth."** (John 4:24) The true meaning of 'Christian Faith' is not merely mental agreement that Jesus is God's Son, who took the penalty due to each of us, died for all of us, and rose from the dead. Faith does not consist of just saying that you believe in Jesus. Believers commit their entire self, mind, heart, body and soul to following after our Good Shepherd, who said, **"I am the way, and the truth, and the life; no one comes to the Father but through Me."** (John 14:6) That is why David, and all believers pray, *"Into your hands I commit my spirit; deliver me, Lord, my faithful God."* (verse 5)

"My life is consumed by anguish and my years by groaning; my strength fails because of my affliction, and my bones grow weak because of all my enemies." (verses 10-11) Living a godly life is often exhausting. We are always warring with enemies within and without. As we age, this warfare wears us down. We suffer **affliction** in our hearts because of our love and concern for so many who refuse to listen and follow after God. Our battle against the ceaseless efforts of Satan to delude,

divide, and to stir up strife never ends. It is certainly a battle as real as any. Without the refreshing strength of the Holy Spirit, we also "***grow weak.***"

"***I trust in you, Lord; I say, "You are my God." My times are in your hands; deliver me from the hands of my enemies, from those who pursue me. Let your face shine on your servant; save me in your unfailing love.***" (verses 14-16) It is not always easy to understand this in the midst of suffering and hardships, but God is aware of what is happening in your life. It is not always because it is His will for it to have happened. Satan is in charge of the evil that happens on earth. He and those who obey him are always brutalizing the innocent. Myriads of believers in Jesus Christ have suffered immensely for our faith. They have been murdered by the millions; and yet, they never denied their faith in their God and Savior. All we can do is to know "***My times are in your hands,***" and to ask for God to save us "*in your unfailing love.*" Do this and know that His Kingdom shall come soon. "**Even so, Come quickly, Lord Jesus.**" (Revelation 22:20)

The righteous, who do not worship Satan, the god of this world, and refuse to seek for temporary pleasures, will always be persecuted. Therefore, David the king says, "***Let the lying lips be mute, which speak arrogantly against the righteous with pride and contempt.***" (verse 18) It hurts to be slandered and accused of wrongs when we are innocent, especially when it comes from those we love and thought loved us. Jesus was slandered too. He was rejected, hated, tortured, and crucified by those he created to become God's children. Even Christ's prayer while hanging on his cross was this, "**Father, forgive them, for they do not know what they are doing.**" (Luke 23:24) This is the Path of Christ and those who believe in Him: Just as He forgave his enemies on the cross and loved them to the end by paying the penalty of their sins on their behalf, we are to die to ourselves and our natural inclinations of our flesh and love our enemies. Yes, we are to pray for them, and to return good for evil.

Even if disease, old age, or enemies overcome us, we do not fear death. "**Therefore, being always of good courage, and knowing that while we are at home in the body we are absent from the Lord— for we walk by faith, not by sight— we are of good courage, I say, and prefer rather to be absent from the body and to be at home with the Lord.**" (2 Corinthians 5:6-8) Death for those who have given themselves wholly to Christ is not the end, but the beginning of a glorious eternal life!

"*Love the Lord, all his faithful people! The Lord preserves those who are true to him, but the proud he pays back in full. Be strong and take heart, all you who hope in the Lord.*" (verses 23-24) Love the Lord! Be true to Him. And God will be with you always. Then, no matter what hardship we encounter, we can be confident and encouraged. We are lifted from despair by hoping in the Lord!

Psalm 32

It is vital that when we read the Holy Scriptures that we do so carefully. "***How blessed is he whose transgression is forgiven; whose sin is covered! How blessed is the man to whom the Lord does not impute iniquity, and in whose spirit there is no deceit!***" (verses 1-2) This psalm begins with a wonderful promise that our sins can be forgiven. Such people receive eternal life in the presence of the Lord, on a new earth with no death, or sorrow. This is the "free gift" that God gives to all mankind through belief in Jesus Christ. Our sins are washed away. God remembers them no more. Our sinful spirit is replaced by the purity of God's Holy Spirit that comes and resides within. Hallelujah!

But let's consider the last few words of the second verse, "***in whose spirit there is no deceit!***" The Book of Acts tells about the first church and the acts of the apostles. In the 5th chapter of Acts, it tells the story of a married couple who tried to deceive the apostles. They sold a tract of land and brought a portion of the sale to the apostles to give to the poor in the church. When Peter asked them if the amount they gave was the whole price they received, they both lied. They became examples to the rest of the Church of the truth and holiness the Lord requires from his followers. "**Didn't it belong to you before it was sold? And after it was sold, wasn't the money at your disposal? What made you think of doing such a thing? You have not lied just to human beings but to God. When Ananias heard this, he fell down and died. And great fear seized all who heard what had happened.**" (Acts 5:3-5) A few hours later his wife came in, told the same lie, and she also fell down and died.

To follow Jesus is to turn away (repent) of our old ways of living, and to seek after holiness. Jesus instructs us to "**Enter through the narrow gate; for the gate is wide and the way is broad that leads to destruction, and there are many who enter through it. For the gate is small and the way is narrow that leads to life, and there are few who find it.**" (Matthew 7:13-14) We go from following after the masses of humanity and being available for any deed our mortal flesh desires, to Jesus being the master of our life. We curtail our desires to live the life of that Jesus calls us to live. We live to please Him, instead of ourselves. This is the Way, the Truth, and the Life that Jesus calls us to follow. We have stopped believing the great lie of the world and of our flesh, that we should "eat, drink, and be merry, for tomorrow we die." Rather, we believe in and follow after the two commands of our Lord, Savior, King, and Master: "**Love the Lord your God with all your heart and with all your soul and with all your mind. This is the first and greatest commandment. And the second is like it: 'Love your neighbor as yourself. All the Law and the Prophets hang on these two commandments.**" (Matthew 22:36-40)

Of course, the process of being changed into the image of Christ is a lifelong process. Never become too discouraged. It is not easy. As often as we fall, we must rise and continue forward. This is the great promise of Christ, **"If we confess our sins, He is faithful and just, that He will forgive us our sins and cleanse us from all unrighteousness."** (1 John 1:9) But if we go on sinning, after coming to Christ, we experience what David did, ***"When I kept silent about my sin, my body wasted away. For day and night Your hand was heavy upon me. My vitality was drained away as with the fever heat of summer. Selah."*** (verses 3-4)

It is important for us to know this, **"O Lord, you have examined my heart and know everything about me. You know when I sit or stand. When far away you know my every thought. You chart the path ahead of me and tell me where to stop and rest. Every moment you know where I am. You know what I am going to say before I even say it. You both precede and follow me and place your hand of blessing on my head."** (Psalm 139:1-5) There is no point in our ever trying to hide from God. There is nothing that is hidden or secreted from His omniscience. Therefore, David confesses what God already knows, ***"I acknowledged my sin to You, and my iniquity I did not hide; I said, "I will confess my transgressions to the Lord"; and You forgave the guilt of my sin."*** (verse 5) This is marvelous and wonderful! Christ has already paid the penalty for our sins. Now, all we must do when we sin is to confess it to God, turn from it, and get back up and follow Jesus. The sins of every man, woman and child have already been forgiven. All we must do is to receive and believe.

"*Therefore, let everyone who is godly pray to You in a time when You may be found.*" (verse 6) Why do people come to believe in Jesus Christ, the image of God in flesh, who opened the door to eternal life for us? The reasons would be far too many for anyone to count. But David gives three reasons, "*You are my hiding place; You preserve me from trouble; You surround me with songs of deliverance. Selah.*" (verse 7)

"*I will instruct you and teach you in the way you should go; I will counsel you with my loving eye on you.*" (verse 8) Heavenly wisdom is a gift from God. We must all be 'born again' and receive "**the Advocate, the Holy Spirit, whom the Father will send in My name.**" (Luke 14:26a) It is the Spirit of God within us that opens our hearts and minds to understand the Holy Scriptures. He unites believers so that we share the same mind and spirit in oneness throughout the ages. Christ instructs his disciples that "**He will teach you all things and will remind you of everything I have told you.**" (Luke 14:26b) David closes this psalm with an exhortation and then encouragement. He strongly urges us to choose the path of the Lord. "*Many are the sorrows of the wicked, but he who trusts in the Lord, lovingkindness shall surround him.*" (verse 10) And he gives us a very encouraging reason why. "*Be glad in the Lord and rejoice, you righteous ones; and shout for joy, all you who are upright in heart.*" (verse 11) In this world we all will have troubles and sorrows. It is an inescapable fact of life. No one escapes from it, not even Jesus. Yet, those who have received the love of God through faith in Christ, His Son, the Savior of the world, are still able to be glad, to rejoice, and shout for joy! This life is a brief gust of wind and then it is over.

The older a person gets the more they come to know this. After this short life comes the Judgement. Those who chose to confess their sins and repent of them, and then accept the forgiveness of God through the salvation that Jesus bought for us by his death on the cross, will not be judged. They will continue to live forever on a perfect world where Christ reigns. Those who refuse to confess their sins, repent, and to follow Jesus will be judged. Be warned! **"For the wages of sin is death; but the gift of God is eternal life through Jesus Christ our Lord."** (Romans 6:23)

Psalm 33

When we give our life to Jesus and trust in Him, we discover what true contentment and joy really is. Therefore, it is only natural for Christians to rejoice, even in the midst of hardships. David begins with, **"Sing for joy in the Lord, O you righteous ones! Praise is becoming to the upright. Give thanks to the Lord with lyre (music.)"** (verses 1-2) Just as we parents relish our children's happiness, and delight when we hear them innocently singing, so too our Father in heaven delights in hearing His children rejoice. It is an endless circle of joy because God is watching over us and we have no need to fear.

"For the word of the Lord is upright, and all His work is done in faithfulness. He loves righteousness and justice. The earth is full of the lovingkindness of the Lord." (verses 4-5) Just as when we were children and had parents who we looked to for protection and to supply all of our needs, we now have a Father in heaven who has perfect love for us. No one could ever come close to having the love for us that Jesus has. He will never let us down. He is our peace, our joy, and our provider. Those who seek Him with all their heart will receive eternal life and experience unending bliss!In verses 6-9 David declares the power of the Almighty. "***By the word of the Lord the heavens were made, and by the breath of His mouth all their host. Let all the earth fear the Lord. Let all the inhabitants of the world stand in awe of Him. For He spoke, and it was done.***" David announces the obvious. God is far greater and more powerful than any man or nation. There is nothing that He cannot do for us. We are so fortunate that God is who He is. The Lord who seeks for us and longs for our affection is a God of mercy, forgiveness, kindness, and love. "**In this the love of God was made manifest among us, that God sent his only Son into the world, so that we might live through him. In this is love, not that we have loved God but that he loved us and sent his Son to be the propitiation for our sins. Beloved, if God so loved us, we also ought to love one another. No one has ever seen God; if we love one another, God abides in us and his love is perfected in us.**" (1 John 4:7-21)

"***Blessed is the nation whose God is the Lord, the people whom He has chosen for His own inheritance.***" (verse 12) Extreme political divides are occurring across the world. Family and friends are divided. This is not happening only in America. This Satan inspired divisiveness, anger, and hatred of those who disagree about public policies and politics, are ripping many nations apart. Christ Himself warned us that, "**Every kingdom divided against itself is brought to desolation, and every city or house divided against itself will not stand.**" (Matthew 12:25) The entire world is being fractured with violence and hatred of our neighbors. Any confessing Christian who joins in with that melee has strayed from the

Path of Life. "*The Lord looks from heaven; He sees all the sons of men; from His dwelling place He looks out on all the inhabitants of the earth.*" (verses 13-14) There is nothing hidden from the eyes of the Lord. He knew the decisions of governments and peoples and the history of our earth before the worlds were formed. With this foreknowledge God formed a plan. That plan is now nearing its completion. Corrupt leaders have always existed and always will. Certainly, that was true in Christ's and the apostles' time too. But we are now at the culmination of this age. Evil, deception and falsehood are have greatly increased. The world seems on the verge of all-out war. – Do not be alarmed. Christ warned us about this. Do not get caught up in this furor. Keep your eyes on Jesus and walk in God's Spirit of love, reconciliation, and truth.

When asked by His disciples what would be the signs of the End, and Christ's establishment of His rule on earth, Jesus answered, "**When you hear of wars and rumors of wars, do not be frightened; those things must take place; but that is not yet the end. For nation will rise up against nation, and kingdom against kingdom; there will be earthquakes in various places; there will also be famines. These things are merely the beginning of birth pangs. "But be on your guard; for they will deliver you to the courts, and you will be flogged in the synagogues, and you will stand before governors and kings for My sake, as a testimony to them.**" (Mark 13:7-9) Christians are called to preach the gospel to all people, especially now, when this world, its rulers and governments are coming to a horrible end. We are not to be participants in hating anyone. Christians have a far greater calling: To show the world the truth of our having an intimate relationship with God by loving everyone and sharing with them the Good News of eternal life through faith in Jesus Christ. Remedying the problems of the world through politics has never worked. It never will. Christians are to preach about the rule of Christ in people lives, not into following after any political philosophy. *"Behold, the eye of the Lord is on those who fear Him, on those who hope for His love and kindness. Our soul waits for the Lord; He is our help and our shield."* (verses 18 & 20) We are to keep our eyes focused on the Lord. This is the description Jesus gave of those who walk in His footsteps, **"They are not of the world, even as I am not of it. Sanctify them by the truth; your word is truth. As you sent me into the world, I have sent them into the world."** (John 17:16-19) Do not get caught up in worldly disputes and divisions. Jesus explained what His divine mission was. It must be ours too. **"The Son of Man did not come to be served, but to serve, and to give his life as a ransom for many."** (Matthew 20:28)

"For our heart rejoices in Him because we trust in His holy name. Let Your lovingkindness, O Lord, be upon us, according as we have hoped in You." (verses 21-22) Our hearts should be focused on one thing, the Lord. Thank Him for his lovingkindness. Rejoice with shouting, songs, dancing, and praise. Believers should never allow anything to separate us from each other; for what separates us from each other also separates us from close fellowship with Jesus. Let us turn away from the concerns of the world that divide our union and focus on loving each other and praising God. *"Sing for joy in the Lord, O you righteous ones. Praise is becoming to the upright."* (verse 1)

Psalm 34

The importance of praise cannot be emphasized enough. Continually, throughout each day, it is good for us to see and realize the things God is doing for us. *"I will bless the Lord at all times; His praise shall continually be in my mouth."* (verse 1) We are encouraged to praise the Lord more than anything else asked of us in the Bible. As we live, let us also see with open eyes what God has and is doing for us daily.

"My soul will make its boast in the Lord; the humble will hear it and rejoice." (verse 2) There are so many millions who live with far less than what we have; and yet, they do not waver from their faith in God. These are the *"humble"* of which the Scriptures speak. It can also refer to those of us who have been more fortunate in being blessed with worldly goods and money; but, it requires us to know that all we have is given to us by the hand of God, not just for ourselves, but for those who are less fortunate than we are too. **"This is pure and undefiled religion, ... to keep ourselves unstained by the world."** (James 1:27) In his New Testament letter, James emphasizes this. **"Listen, my beloved brothers, has not God chosen those who are poor in the world to be rich in faith**

and heirs of the kingdom, which he has promised to those who love him? But you have dishonored the poor man. Are not the rich the ones who oppress you, and the ones who drag you into court?" (James 2: 5-6) If God has been generous to us, it is a blessing; but it also may be a curse that will lead our hearts away from the Truth. Too often, the poor are persecuted by the wealthy. It has always been so. The sinful nature of our humanity craves to feel superior to others. Wealth puts people in a position of great advantage. And many of them think that the poor are cursed and deserve to be less fortunate than themselves. People frequently look upon them with contempt and disdain. Beware! Do not permit your soul to lift itself up and think more highly of yourself than you do for all others. Pride of riches will eat away at your faith until it is in rags and worthless. **"To fear the LORD is to hate evil; I hate pride and arrogance, evil behavior and perverse speech."** (Proverbs 8:13)

"O magnify the Lord with me and let us exalt His name together." (verse 3) Perhaps here on earth, until the Lord's return, there is nothing that delights the Lord more than a gathering of believers singing praises to Him. Nor is there anything on earth that draws us closer together as Believers than when we do so. This intimate unity is to be cherished. We should not spend our time on earth involving ourselves in earthly matters, but we should devote ourselves to loving all people and sharing with them the Truth of God.

"I sought the Lord, and He answered me, and delivered me from all my fears." (verse 4) There are many things that can hurt us. There are many reasons for us to be afraid; war, drought,

famine, disease, disasters, injury, the economy, death… There is no firm security here. Even the tremendously wealthy are afraid and are always scrambling to get richer, to protect what they have, and to never experience hardship. Anything can happen at any time over which we have no control that can harm or destroy us. And as we enter into these 'Last days' the causes for us to be fearful will increase dramatically! But believers should be courageous when the hearts of unbelievers fail. It is our testimony. So that we do not become like those around us, shaking with trepidation, Jesus assures us that we can have peace. "**I have told you these things, so that in me you may have peace. In this world you will have trouble. But take heart! I have overcome the world.**" (John 16:33) David was always able to overcome fear by remembering that God was with him; and that whatever happens, God will always be with him. When the Almighty God of love and kindness walks with us there is no reason to be afraid. Therefore, David says, "*I sought the Lord, and He answered me, and delivered me from all my fears.*" (verse 4)

Poverty, and the fear of not having the basic necessities to keep alive is the most common fear among mankind. That is why people are driven to gain more and more money. Riches are the god in which they trust. About this, the Apostle Paul says, "**For the love of money is the root of all evil: which while some coveted after, they have erred from the faith, and pierced themselves through with many sorrows.**" (1 Timothy 6:10)) Wars between nations and fights among people are all due to selfish greed. We all want what we want and will not stop until we get it. Among Christians this is never to be. Instead, we are always to trust in the Lord and to be content with what He gives us. Do not desire the riches of this world; but, long for and seek after God. David exhorts us, "***O taste and see that the Lord is good; how blessed is the man who takes refuge in Him! O fear the Lord, you His saints; for to those who fear Him there is no want. The young lions do lack and suffer hunger; but they who seek the Lord shall not be in want of any good thing.***" (verses 8-10)

This is the wisdom that responds to man's fears, "***Come, you children, listen to me; I will teach you the fear of the Lord. Who is the man who desires life and loves length of days that he may see good? Keep your tongue from evil and your lips from speaking deceit. Depart from evil and do good; seek peace and pursue it. The eyes of the Lord are toward the righteous and His ears are open to their cry.***" (verses 11-14) Let us seek the Lord with all of our strength; for He alone is to be feared. To live in sin is to live in a state of blind ignorance and fear. But when we live to please the Lord, we have peace. "***The righteous cry, and the Lord hears and delivers them out of all their troubles.***" (verse 17) David concludes this psalm with, "***Evil shall slay the wicked, and those who hate the righteous will be condemned.***" (verse 21) There is a day reserved for all of us to be judged. Did we take refuge in the Lord, and seek Him to be our Protector and our Shield? Did we love and treat all others with kindness and the love of God? Or did we decide to live according to our own rules? -- This is all that matters. "***The Lord redeems the soul of His servants, and none of those who take refuge in Him will be condemned.***" (verse 22)

Psalm 35

We all have enemies, sometimes members of our own families, or lifelong friends. Even fellow Christians will attack us for other than godly reasons. This is a reality of life. None is perfect. Anger, due to others' disappointments and frustrations can be directed at us despite our complete innocence. Hatred is an extraordinarily strong emotion. Its heat is hotter than an oven. It is where murder comes from. We are permitted as Christians to hate sin, but not those who practice sin. We are to have compassion, love, and understanding. Are they not also our brothers and sisters? Genetic science has confirmed that we are all related and came from the same two parents, Adam and Eve, as the Bible claims?"***Contend, O Lord, with those who contend with me; fight against those who fight against me.***" (verse 1) It has been necessary for many of us to pray this same prayer occasionally. False accusations and undeserved attacks are naturally emotionally painful. It causes anger and resentment to arise in us. Therefore, learn to leave our response in God's hands. Our calling is to love and to help sinners. If we genuinely want to be "children of God" then we must overlook the faults of others. "**You have heard that it was said, 'You shall love your neigh-**

bor and hate your enemy.' "But I say to you, love your enemies and pray for those who persecute you, so that you may be sons of your Father who is in heaven." (Matthew 5:43-44)

"Let those be turned back and humiliated who devise evil against me. Let them be like chaff before the wind, with the angel of the Lord driving them on. Let their way be dark and slippery, with the angel of the Lord pursuing them. For without cause, they hid their net for me; without cause, they dug a pit for my soul." (verses 5-7) These are the ones of whom David speaks; for, it is humans inspired by fleshly lusts and devilish spirits who do evil things. We get caught in the nets they set for us that lead away from the Path of Truth. It is vital for Christians to walk through life led by God's Holy Spirit. Share Christ's love and our love with unbelievers; but do not live as they do. If we do, then we sin and bring shame to our testimony about the redemption of our Blessed Lord. **"Do not be misled: Bad company corrupts good character. Come back to your senses as you ought and stop sinning; for there are some who are ignorant of God—I say this to your shame."** (1 Corinthians 33:34)Read your Bible, find a good fellowship of Believers and join them in prayer, praise, and learning God's will through the Holy Scriptures. Jesus said the 'Word' was nourishment for our souls. Which brings me to an anecdote many have heard: "An 1800's missionary was travelling around America preaching the Gospel to native American tribes. When he returned to these tribes, he always asked what their faith was like. An old Cherokee Chief told him, "It is like a fight to the death between two dogs within me, a black dog, and a white dog." So, the preacher asked, "Which one is

winning?" To which the Chief simply replied, "The one I feed the most."

Jesus said that in the last days, **"Because lawlessness is increased, most people's love will grow cold."** (Matthew 24:12) And Jesus claimed that **"Brother will betray brother to death, and a father his child. Children will rebel against their parents and have them put to death."** (Mark 13:12) As evil increases during our times, we must be all the more diligent to study God's Bible. It is the holy words of the only true God. They are words of love, mercy, and forgiveness. This is what David declares will be his exultant proclamation when he is delivered from his accusers. *"And my soul shall rejoice in the Lord; it shall exult in His salvation. All my bones will say, "Lord, who is like You, who delivers the afflicted from him who is too strong for him, and the afflicted and the needy from him who robs him?"* (verses 9-10)

Those who trust in the Maker of heaven and earth are given the gift of God's Holy Spirit to indwell them, to lead them in the Path of God. Those who refuse to do so and choose to believe that this life is all that there is, who do not believe in nor trust in a kind and loving Creator, are controlled by the spirit of the god of the unbelieving, the Devil. Their lives will suffer the consequences, now or later. **"Your enemy the devil prowls around like a roaring lion looking for someone to devour."** (1 Peter 5: 8) Since they do not believe in God, they have no refuge and protection from our greatest enemy.

"They repay me evil for good, to the bereavement of my soul." (verse 12) Despite all circumstances that we encounter and

must endure, know that the love of God within us is far stronger and more powerful than the hate in others. Loving others is our witness. It the testimony we live. We are always continuing to love and to forgive. It is a sign to people that we are indeed the children of Heaven's Holy One. **"A new commandment I give you: Love one another. As I have loved you, so also you must love one another. By this all men will know that you are My disciples, if you love one another."** (John 13:34-35) It is our duty to live in a manner that proves that this is true. "**If you forgive anyone, I also forgive him. And if I have forgiven anything, I have forgiven it in the presence of Christ for your sake, in order that Satan should not outwit us. For we are not unaware of his schemes."** (2 Corinthians 2:10) How can others believe that God loves and forgives them unless we show them by continuing to love and to forgive. We have been saved from death and entered into eternal life and into all the pleasures of God. Now, we live not for ourselves but for others. Our lives are no longer our own. Our lives belong to Christ, to serve Him by serving others.

*"**Lord, how long will You look on? Rescue my soul from their ravages, my only life from the lions.**"* (verse 17) Bible believing Christians who have searched the holy promises know this answer to David's inquiry, "***How long?***" There will be no earthly peace for believers until our Lord returns and reigns supreme. Jesus promised us, "**But you, brothers, are not in the darkness so that this day should overtake you like a thief. For you are all sons of the light and sons of the day…**" (1 Thessalonians 5:4-5) These are the final days on earth. It is a sin for us to keep the knowledge of how to have an intimate

and eternal relationship with their righteous Maker. Now is the time for all Christians to publicly declare their faith!

"Let them shout for joy and rejoice, who favor my vindication; and let them say continually, "The Lord be magnified, who delights in the prosperity of His servant." And my tongue shall declare Your righteousness and Your praise all day long." (verses 27–28) The joy of good parents when they bear a new child is very comparable to the joy we experience when God uses us to bring another person to trust in Jesus Christ. We rejoice with them, and we rejoice for ourselves too! We are now partakers of the greatest gift of God: Righteousness; for only the righteous shall see God and spend eternity in His presence, knowing the fullness of joy! **"Just so, I tell you, there is joy before the angels of God over one sinner who repents."** (Luke 15:10)

We are all sinners. Everyone can be forgiven of their sins, washed clean by the Spirit of God, and walk in a manner that shows we are indeed reborn as God's beloved. This is free to all who will believe it. And when you do, you will rejoice and experience a liberty you have never known.

Psalm 36

"*I have a message from God in my heart concerning the sinfulness of the wicked: There is no fear of God before their eyes.*" (verse 1) Three things are given to all Christians to empower them to overcome "sinfulness": faith, hope, and love. With true faith also comes a *"fear of God."* Just as children should fear transgressing the rules of their earthly father, we should know that our heavenly Father also will discipline us if we stray. With faith also comes righteous living. ""**But if we walk in the light, as he is in the light, we have fellowship with one another, and the blood of Jesus his Son cleanses us from all sin.**" (1 John 1:7)) After that, the work of the Holy Spirit begins. And as we grow in the Spirit of the Lord there comes love. We begin to care about those around us more than we do for ourselves. The love of God manifests itself from within us. -- This is the Christian's life experience.

In the rest of this psalm's first stanza there is a warning. "*The words of his mouth are wickedness and deceit; he has ceased to be wise and to do good. He plans wickedness upon his bed; he sets himself on a path that is not good; he does not despise evil.*" (verse 3–4) We all have the freedom of choice to do this. One must continue choosing to believe in and to walk with God. "**Now the just shall live by faith; but if any man draws back, my soul shall have no pleasure in him.**" (Hebrews 10:38) Jesus encourages us "**Be faithful until death, and I will give you the crown of life.**" (Revelation 2:10) As Christians, we must always seek to remain in the Spirit of God. If we do not, we will fall back into obeying our fleshly, carnal desires; and become as David says, "*He sets himself on a path that is not good; he does not despise evil.*" (verse 4)

Now, David turns from warning to praise, "*O Lord, You preserve man and beast. How precious is Your lovingkindness, O God! And the children of men take refuge in the shadow of Your wings.*" (verses 6–7) These are some of the primary reasons most Christians do not turn away from believing in the Word of God. Their own personal experiences of preservation, love, kindness, and having a place of refuge, peace, and comfort in the midst of the trails upon this earth. "*They drink their fill of the abundance of Your house; and You give them to drink of the river of Your delights.*" (verse 8)

"*For with You is the fountain of life; in Your light we see light.*" (verse 9) No one can mistake the difference between light and dark, except for the blind. This is true physically and spiritually. The times that many people come to Christ is when they are in deep affliction, and trouble. Darkness comes in many ways into our lives. It envelopes us. "**Jesus spoke to them, saying, "I am the light of the world. Whoever follows me will not walk in darkness but will have the light of life.**" (John 8:12)

This is the central verse of this psalm, "*O continue Your lovingkindness to those who know You, and Your righteousness to the upright in heart.*" (verse 10) Christians never leave the Lord because of God's love and kindness. He clothes us with it and makes it flourish within us. He cleanses us from our sinful ways and sets our feet on a straight and narrow path to eternal life. He is our shelter amid life's storms. Therefore, we pray with David these words, "*Let not the foot of pride come upon me and let not the hand of the wicked drive me away. There the doers of iniquity have fallen; they have been thrust down and cannot rise.*" (verses 11–12). It is important that we remind ourselves, and those with whom we fellowship, to walk in the Spirit, because *"the fruit of the Spirit is love, joy, peace, forbearance, kindness, goodness, faithfulness, gentleness and self-control. Against such things there is no law. Now those who belong to Christ Jesus have crucified the flesh with its passions and desires. If we live by the Spirit, let us also walk by the Spirit. Let us not become boastful, challenging one another, envying one another."* (Galatians 5:22–26)

The "*foot of pride*" will always, as David says, "*drive me away.*" (verse 11) If we permit this to happen then David tells us plainly, "*There the doers of iniquity have fallen; they have been thrust down and cannot rise.*" (verse 12)

Psalm 37

David became a wealthy man and a king over Israel and Judah. He received massive tributes from local nations of gold, silver, bronze, precious stones, and timber. He was not in need of anything. However, while growing up, David and his family were among the smallest of the Jewish tribes. He had been a poor shepherd and had known deprivation. And as a young man, he was always hiding from King Saul, in caves in the desert. David knew what poverty and hunger were, and the hardships of the poor. He had suffered at the hands of a rich and a powerful king. He shares with us the wisdom he has learned: "***Do not fret because of evildoers, be not envious toward wrongdoers. For they will wither quickly like the grass and fade like the green herb.***" (verse 1–2) He is teaching to his people a lesson he had learned in life, a lesson he continually repeats, and which is frequently confirmed by other authors of the Bible, "***Do not be envious.***" (verse 1) He teaches us to be content with what the Lord provides us. Let us never covet what another has been given. Do not complain about the grace God has given us by wanting what others have. Thank God for what He has given to us and be content. "***Trust in the Lord and do good; dwell in the land and cultivate*** *faithfulness. Delight yourself in the Lord; and He will give you the desires of your heart."* (verse 3–4)

As in many of David's Psalms, he contrasts the differences between the righteous, and the blessings they will receive; versus the wicked, and the horrible judgements that will befall them. He does this as encouragement and as a warning for his people, and for us. In this psalm the contrasts are many. Let's focus only on what to do to receive blessings, instead of curses.

"Trust in the Lord; do good; cultivate faithfulness." (verse 3) The meaning of the word "cultivate" is to: "till, plow, dig, hoe, farm, work, fertilize, mulch, and weed." In this way, all Christians are farmers. Our farms are ourselves. The Lord's command is for us to work hard at doing good and at developing a right relationship with Him. -- Farmers must trust in the Lord. The right weather and soil and water for producing a bounty of nutritional sustenance are not totally in the farmer's control. Consequently, they are usually humble people who rely on the grace and favor of God to make it through each season. So too, should we be.

"Delight yourself in the Lord; commit your way; trust also in Him. Rest in the Lord; wait patiently; do not fret." (verses 6–7) No one can experience "*delight*" if they are anxious. Think of when you were a child and your parents told you, "Don't be afraid. I am right here with you. Everything is OK." This is what God is saying to us all through the Bible! "Just trust me. Relax. Wait and see. There is nothing to be afraid of when I am with you." Like good earthly parents, our heavenly Father and our Lord want us to be happy and at peace.

Godly people learn this vital lesson, which is critical to walking closely with the Lord: "***Rest in the Lord and wait patiently for Him***" (verse 7) Happiness will not be found for long if we do not have enough faith and trust in our Lord's love for us that we lose confidence in His promises. The Christian walk is filled with waiting. That is how the Lord expands our faith and draws us closer and closer to Him.

I used to worry about being poor. I worked 17 hours a day for many years, every day, scrambling to avoid it. Then one day the Spirit made me stop and meditate upon this verse, "**It is useless for you to work so hard from early morning until late at night, anxiously working for food to eat; for God gives rest to his loved ones.**" (Psalm 127:2) I am telling you the truth, when I stopped working myself almost to death, everything in my life got better, not worse. And the Lord blessed us with many times more income than when I was trusting in many hours of labor, instead of in his loving providence.

"*He is gracious and lends.*" (verse 26) When we know that it is the Lord who is providing for us and paying us for our labors, then we can lend in confidence. When we realize that all we have is from the merciful hand of God, then we no longer think of what we possess as ours, but His. Therefore, we can obey this command of Jesus without any worry. "**Love your enemies, and do good, and lend, expecting nothing in return; and your reward will be great, and you will be sons of the Most High; for He Himself is kind to ungrateful and evil men.**" (Luke 6:35) If it hurts a bit for us to give when asked, consider it a greater blessing. Your reward from the Lord for doing so will be greater too. Some Christians tithe regularly and figure that they have fulfilled God's will and need to give no more. But that is not what Jesus commanded us to do from the beginning. "**If there is a poor man among your brothers within any of the gates in the land that the LORD your God is giving you, you are not to harden your heart or shut your hand from your poor brother. Instead, you are to open your hand to him and freely loan him whatever he needs.**" (Deuteronomy 15:7–8) One can only do this if they have faith. And as we do those things God desires, He promises, "*He will give you the desires of your heart;* and "*Bring forth your righteousness as the light.* (verses 7–9)

David lists many blessings in this psalm to strongly encourage his people to trust in Jehovah. "*The humble will inherit the land and will delight themselves in abundant prosperity. The Lord knows the days of the blameless, and their inheritance will be forever. They will not be ashamed in the time of evil, and in the days of famine they will have abundance. The steps of a man are established by the Lord, and He delights in his way. When he falls, he will not be hurled headlong, because the Lord is the One who holds his hand. They are preserved forever. His steps do not slip. The Lord will not leave him in his hand or let him be condemned when he is judged. Wait for the Lord and keep His way, and He will exalt you to inherit the land; when the wicked are cut off, you will see it. Mark the blameless man and behold the upright; the man of peace will have a posterity. He is their strength in time of trouble. The Lord helps them and delivers them; He delivers them from the wicked and saves them.*" (verses 11, 18–40)

The essence of Solomon's wisdom, David's son, is summed up in 'Fear God. Work hard. And be content.' He repeats this in many ways. Perhaps he learned it from reading this psalm of his father's. *"Better is the little of the righteous than the abundance of many wicked."* (verse 16) This wisdom is contrary to that of the world. **"Do not work to be rich, cease from seeking it. If you seek it, it will fly away. Surely it will make wings for itself like an eagle and will fly into the sky.** (Proverbs 23–4-5) The Apostle Paul reasserts this, **"Work hard and cheerfully at all you do, just as though you were working for the Lord and not merely for your masters, remembering that it is the Lord Christ who is going to pay you, giving you your full portion of all he owns. He is the one you are really working for. And if you do not do your best for him, he will pay you in a way that you won't like—for he has no special favorites who can get away with shirking."** (Colossians 3:23–25)

The type of work is not important, as long as it is work that is honoring to our Lord. Laziness is never honoring to God. Christians should be diligent in working to meet the physical needs of their family, of the church, and of the poor. They should also be diligent in meeting the spiritual needs of themselves and of others. Christians who do not work for their daily sustenance are not to be fed by those of us that do (unless because of injury, age, or disability). **"For also when we were with you, this we commanded you, that if anyone does not wish to work, neither let him eat. For we hear some among you are walking disorderly, not working at all but being busybodies."** (2 Thessalonians 3.10–12)

So many people seek to avoid work. Even when they are hired to do a job, they hide during the day and do nothing, or they do as little as they can. They cheat their employers with dishonest labor. This will lead to poverty. "**A little sleep, a little slumber, a little folding of the hands to rest, and poverty will come upon you like a robber, and want like an armed man.**" (Proverbs 6:10) This also applies to us spiritually. If we do not apply ourselves to prayer, praise, gratitude, reading His word, and fellowship with other Believers, then we will rot on the vine and bear no fruit for the Lord. It is vital that we set times every day when we will take time to "***cultivate faithfulness.***" For if we take refuge in Him, we will receive "***the salvation and the righteous from the Lord; He is their strength in time of trouble. The Lord helps them and delivers them; He delivers them from the wicked and saves them, because they take refuge in Him.***" (verses 39-40)

The day is coming when we will work no longer and enter into our rest. Until that day, we persevere, and we wait, while trusting in God and doing good. "***For evildoers will be cut off, but those who wait for the Lord, they will inherit the land. Yet a little while and the wicked man will be no more; and you will look carefully for his place and he will not be there. But the humble will inherit the land and will delight themselves in abundant prosperity.***" (verse 9-11)

Psalm 38

Learning to be careful and not to sin is a lifetime effort. God helps us in this in many ways. But when we stray from His path, there are frequently consequences. "*O Lord, rebuke me not in Your wrath, and chasten me not in Your burning anger.*" (verse 1) The Lord is our Father. He loves us and wants us to be filled with joy in His presence forever; therefore he "**rebukes**" and "**chastens**" us when we begin to fall away from following Him. All Christians who seek earnestly for the Lord experience this. The Lord lives! He will correct us when we go astray because His heart's desire is for us to live with Him, forever.

If we are truly "born again," then we will suffer when we continue in sin. "*For my iniquities are gone over my head; as a heavy burden they weigh too much for me.*" (verse 4) "*I am benumbed and badly crushed; I groan because of the agitation of my heart.*" (verse 8) This feeling is as bad as David makes it sound. Once felt, you never want to feel it again. It spurs us on to repent and to get back on the "straight and narrow path" that leads to Life everlasting.

"*My heart throbs, my strength fails me; and the light of my eyes, even that has gone from me. My loved ones and my friends stand aloof from my plague; and my kinsmen stand afar off. Those who seek my life lay snares for me."* (verses 10-12) Sinning affects our personality and our face's countenance. It makes us weak. The light of our eyes becomes dim. Loved ones see this and stay away from us in their confusion about our change of behavior and manners. Our enemies see this as an opportune time to attack us. – This is another incentive for not walking away from our Good Shepherd and following always after Him.

"For I said, "May they not rejoice over me, who, when my foot slips, would magnify themselves against me." For I am ready to fall, and my sorrow is continually before me. For I confess my iniquity; I am full of anxiety because of my sin." (verses 16-18) David has committed a sin and confessed it. Now, his enemies are using it to try and bring him down. His adversaries continue to *"threatened destruction, and they devise treachery all day long."*

Despite how much we love and work to make others' lives better, some will not regard our kindness. They will take any occasion to accuse us when we stumble and do something unwise or foolish. David claims that this is *"because I follow what is good."* (verse 20) We who seek after our Maker, to do the things that please Him, rather than the desires of our flesh, inevitably will have enemies. Just as the Holy Spirit convicts us of sin, we by our love and good works convict others of their ungodly behavior.

David then quits his complaint and remembers the promises of God. *"I hope in You, O Lord; You will answer, O Lord my*

God." (verse 15) This verse is evidence of David's long relationship with the Lord. He has sinned before. He probably will again; but when he does, David hopes in God's love and mercy. David revives his confidence as he says, ***"Do not forsake me, O Lord! O my God do not be far from me! Make haste to help me, O Lord, my salvation!"*** (verses 21-22)

Our God is for us, not against us. He does not seek to judge us. He has done everything He can to wipe away all of our sins and to forgive us. He has done so because He loves us thoroughly. So, when we sin, remember these wonderful words of encouragement. **"If we confess our sins, he is faithful and just and will forgive us our sins and purify us from all unrighteousness."** (1 John 1:9)

Psalm 39

In this psalm we hear David bemoaning his lack of control over his tongue and his anger, particularly when he is in the company of those who are wicked, to whom David's life must be a witness. "**I said, "I will guard my ways that I may not sin with my tongue; I will guard my mouth as with a muzzle while the wicked are in my presence." I was mute and silent, I refrained even from good, and my sorrow grew worse. My heart was hot within me, while I was musing the fire burned; then I spoke with my tongue.**" (verse 1-3) The bible warns us that "**Everyone must be quick to hear, slow to speak and slow to anger; for the anger of man does not achieve the righteousness of God.**" (James 1:19-20) How often have we all failed at this?

Humility is the first step to our learning to control our tongue. "***Lord, make me to know my end and what is the extent of my days; let me know how transient I am. "Behold, You have made my days as handbreadths, and my lifetime as nothing in Your sight; surely every man at his best is a mere breath. Selah.***" (verses 4-5)

No material things we have on earth will be of any value to us when we die. "***Surely every man walks about as a phantom;***

surely they make an uproar for nothing; he amasses riches and does not know who will gather them." (verse 6) Since this is true, David asks why he continues seeking heavenly rewards, rather than enjoying the things he saw most others doing all around him: eating, drinking, and having parties. *"And now, Lord, for what do I wait?"* (verse 7)

David answers his own rhetorical question. *"My hope is in You."* (verse 7b) David does not crave the pleasures of earth. He seeks, and he waits for heavenly rewards. But the wickedness and folly of those about him make David temporarily become despondent and lose hope; for, he is a sinner too.

There is no hope without God. David cannot redeem himself from his own sins; nor can he make himself holy by the strength of his will. David waits for the Lord to hear, to forgive, and to cleanse him of his guilt. He humbles himself before God and confesses his sins; and asks for God's assistance. *"Deliver me from all my transgressions; make me not the reproach of the foolish."* (verse 8)

David knows that seeking after worldly pleasures is vanity, as his son, Solomon emphasized in his writings. **"I have seen everything that is done under the sun, and behold, all is vanity and a striving after wind."** (Ecclesiastes 1:14) Therefore, David pleads, *"make me not the reproach of the foolish."* (verse 8) He is sitting among unbelievers, listening to their vain talk and ideas. As he does, his anger grows *"hot within me, while I was musing the fire burned; then I spoke with my tongue: "Lord, make me to know my end and what is the extent of my days; let me know how transient I am."* (verse 3-4)

David feels the admonishment of God's Holy Spirit convicting him. Instead of being a light to the darkness of his associates, David has allowed himself to become foolish by his silence. ***"I have become mute. I do not open my mouth."*** (verse 9) When we are slipping in our faith, sometimes the Lord allows it to continue until we are repulsed by our own sins. David says, ***"…because it is You who have done it. With reproofs You chasten a man for iniquity; You consume as a moth what is precious to him; surely every man is a mere breath. Selah."*** (verse 10b-11)

Our purpose in this brief life is to seek God and His righteousness. Jesus instructed us, **"Do not store up for yourselves treasures on earth, where moths and vermin destroy, and where thieves break in and steal. But store up for yourselves treasures in heaven, where moths and vermin do not destroy, and where thieves do not break in and steal. For where your treasure is, there your heart will be also."** (Matthew 6: 19-22) In this world, before the coming of our Righteous King, mortal mankind is seeking after as much comfort and pleasure as he can acquire before he dies. The temptation of our eyes attracts us to seeking after the things of the natural world, rather than the things of the spiritual realm. David has lapsed into sitting and listening to foolish men boast about their vanity and folly. This is why the Lord is chastening him.

Because of the curse of Adam and Eve, we must labor to sustain our lives. We must work to earn what we can for ourselves and our loved ones. This can be deceiving and convince us that by our own efforts we have what we have. If we are well-to-do, we take pride in accomplishing it and think of ourselves as better than those who have much less. If we are poor, then we covet the things that others have, and we do not. These thoughts arise from our undegenerated self. Both of these attitudes are sinful. God has chosen some to be rich and others to have less.

Rich or poor, either can be a blessing or a curse. It is a considered a curse if we are poor, but that is not how God sees it. Being in daily need is a much greater blessing than having no needs or wants at all, because it drives us to our knees every day. We are totally dependent on God's grace and His providence.

Brothers, and sisters, let us seek the Lord before the things this world has to offer. In the world there is no security. So many things can happen to suddenly turn our lives upside down. "*My lifetime is as nothing in Your sight; surely every man at his best is a mere breath.*" (verse 5) There can be found no real and lasting peace and contentment without a relationship with the One who transcends this world, created it, and sustains all the life of this planet by his mercy. The Lord is our sole provider and sustainer. We must humble ourselves before Him in gratitude for what we have and be content. "**If that is how God clothes the grass of the field, which is here today and tomorrow is thrown into the fire, will he not much more clothe you – you of little faith? So do not worry, saying, 'What shall we eat?' or 'What shall we drink?' or 'What shall we wear?' For the pagans run after all these things, and your heavenly Father knows that you need them. But seek first his kingdom and his righteousness, and all these things will be given to you as well.**" (Matthew 6:30-33)

We really must take the 'long view' about Life. This time on earth is a challenge given to all of us. Will we live just for the number of years destined for us, seeking solely to make our life as easy and as painless as possible before we die? Or will we choose to work and construct a life of great value to others, which results in eternal life?

We have all heard the saying, "The person with the most toys when they dies wins!" The Bible disagrees. We are to live for God everyday so that we pass this test and graduate into a wonderful, everlasting reality. David knows this. He asks God to forgive his sins and not to abandon him to merely a life on this earth. David has confessed his sins and humbled himself before the one and only living God. "***Hear my prayer, O Lord, and give ear to my cry; do not be silent at my tears; for I am a stranger with You, a sojourner like all my fathers.***" (verse 12) To "sojourn" is to stay somewhere temporarily. David knew that this earthly life is short. Therefore, he pleads for his Savior, "***Turn Your gaze away from me, that I may smile again before I depart and am no more.***" (verse 13) It is our lifting up prayers of contrition with humility to our holy Maker that we are forgiven and are welcomed into God's eternal kingdom.

Psalm 40

This is certainly one of my personal favorites of David's Psalms. In my daily prayer, I frequently find myself quoting from this psalm. I can profoundly identify with every line, beginning with the first. "***I waited patiently for the Lord; and He inclined to me and heard my cry.***" (verse 1).

I began life as a Christian, at least as far back as memory takes me. Neither of my parents were Christians, but my grandmother was. Every Sunday, she would take me to the First Baptist Church of Santa Ana, CA. I think I was 4 when a teacher in my Sunday school class shared about Jesus. It struck me like a bolt of lightning! My heart broke and my body began shaking. Tears flowed heavily down my face until I could bear it no more. "Jesus! Jesus! I want Jesus!" I cried out with a passion and desperation I had never known. At my interruption, she stopped, turned the class over to another teacher, and took me into the hallway, where we sat together in an alcove. We prayed together and I was born-again. I knew at that early age that my calling was to be a pastor and preacher.

My belief in Christ as my Creator, Lord and Savior, has never wavered. But as the hurts and hardships of life mounted-up I became overwhelmed and depressed. I began making friends with unbelievers and practicing ungodly behaviors. The joy of my salvation disappeared. It was then, like David, that I called out and cried to God with the full sincerity of my heart and being, "Save me!" Like David in this psalm I cried out "***Be pleased, O Lord, to deliver me; make haste, O Lord, to help me.***" (verse 13) – Then, "***I waited patiently for the Lord; and He inclined to me and heard my cry.***" (verse 1) There was an immediate change in my heart; but it took a while to repent of all the bad habits I had developed.

God put an earnest desire of repentance in my heart and replaced the rebellion that had been there. I can now honestly testify that what David says happened to him, also happened to me. "***He brought me up out of the pit of destruction, out of the miry clay, and He set my feet upon a rock making my footsteps firm. He put a new song in my mouth, a song of praise to our God.***" (verse 2-3) Having witnessed this life changing event and recommitting myself to Jesus Christ as my Lord and Master, I have been filled with the fire and passion to tell others of God's patience and mercy; and to be the pastor and preacher God always wanted me to be. Now, my hope is, "***Many will see and fear and will trust in the Lord.***" (verse 3b)

With all my heart and being I also can declare, "***Many, O Lord my God, are the wonders which You have done, and Your thoughts toward us; there is none to compare with You. If I would declare and speak of them, they would be too numerous to count.***" (verse 5) My heart and mind have been changed. Rather than focusing on my life's hardships and difficulties, it is the innumerable blessings of my Lord that I count and for which I am continually uttering praise.

This is another psalm that can also be heard as the voice of Jesus. Certainly, David is writing under the influence of the Holy Spirit and prophecy and in the voice of Christ when he writes, "*Then I said, "Behold, I come; in the scroll of the book it is written of me. I delight to do Your will, O my God; your Law is within my heart." I have proclaimed glad tidings of righteousness in the great congregation; behold, I will not restrain my lips, O Lord, You know. I have not hidden Your righteousness within my heart; I have spoken of Your faithfulness and Your salvation; I have not concealed Your lovingkindness and Your truth from the great congregation.*" (verse 7-10) As it is the testimony of Christ, so it is to be ours too.

As we grow in the Spirit of the Lord, we become increasingly confident and certain of His presence with us, in all circumstances of our lives. "*You, O Lord, will not withhold Your compassion from me, Your lovingkindness and Your truth will continually preserve me.*" (verse 11) We can, with the Apostle Paul, also proclaim to others, "**God shall supply all your need according to his riches in glory by Christ Jesus.**" (Philippians 4:19)

When we face troubles in life, we can cry out with confidence that the Lord hears us. "*Since I am afflicted and needy, let the Lord be mindful of me. You are my help and my deliverer; do not delay, O my God.*" (verse 17) He will respond to such a plea from his loved ones. Begin to think of all the things for which to thank God. Count His blessings. Praise Him. When it seems that darkness surrounds us, the ever-loving light of God's Spirit dwells within us. So, together with David, we sing to our Savior, "***Let all who seek You rejoice and be glad in You; let those who love Your salvation say continually, "The Lord be magnified!***" (verse 16)

Psalm 41

Once again, David is afraid of his enemies, and he and feeling "***helpless***." His enemies are slandering him, including a close friend who has deceived and abandoned him. So, David begins by counting the blessings of his true friend, the Lord. "***How blessed is he who considers the helpless; the Lord will deliver him in a day of trouble. The Lord will protect him and keep him alive, and he shall be called blessed upon the earth; and do not give him over to the desire of his enemies. The Lord will sustain him upon his sickbed; in his illness, You restore him to health.***" (verses 1-3)

This is every Christian's calling, to manifest our friendship with God by being a friend to all. "**The spirit of the Lord God is upon me, for the Lord has anointed me; he has sent me to bring good news to the afflicted, to bind up the brokenhearted, to proclaim liberty to the captives, and to set the prisoners free; to proclaim the year of God's favor and the day of our God's reckoning; to comfort all mourners, to give them beauty for ashes, the oil of joy in the place of mourning, a song of praise instead of the spirit of sorrow, that they may be called trees of righteousness, the planting**

of the Lord, wherewith he may be glorified." (Isaiah 61:1-3 & Luke 4:14-30) This was the first sermon Jesus gave at the start of His ministry. He proclaims His purpose for his life. His purpose should be ours' too. "**This is my commandment, that you love one another as I have loved you. Greater love has no one than this, that someone lay down his life for his friends.**" (John 15:12)

David then makes his plea, "*O Lord, be gracious to me; heal my soul, for I have sinned against You.*" Before accusing his enemies and 'friend,' David takes personal responsibility and confesses that he has sinned. We are usually the cause of our own problems. We can incite enemies and offend friends without even being aware that we have. Our best intentions do not always bear pleasing fruit. Even though, it does not excuse those who have reacted by devising plans to hurt David. "*All who hate me whisper together against me; against me they devise my hurt.*" (verse 7)

"*My enemies speak evil against me, "When will he die, and his name perish?" And when he comes to see me, he speaks falsehood; his heart gathers wickedness to itself; when he goes outside, he tells it.*" (verses 4-6) In life we encounter people that the Bible refers to as "**sons of disobedience**" (2 Thessalonians 2:3) who delight in being deceptive. Among my associates that come and go there seems always to be some who are false friends and flatterers. No matter how much we love some and give completely of ourselves, not everyone will appreciate it. We all experience wolves in sheep's clothing sometimes in our lives. They betray our trust and our sincere affections and leave us astonished and heart broken. *"And when he comes to see me, he speaks falsehood; his heart gathers wickedness to itself…Even my close friend in whom I trusted, who ate my bread, has lifted up his heel against me."* (verses 6 & 9)

Once again, David, the prophet speaks through the Spirit of Christ. *"But You, O Lord, be gracious to me and raise me up, that I may repay them. By this I know that You are pleased with me, because my enemy does not shout in triumph over me. As for me, you uphold me in my integrity, and You set me in Your presence forever."* (verses 10-12) Many of the hardships, trials, and troubles we experience were also felt by Christ. He too had friends and associates that hurt and betrayed him, even those that sought his life. They repaid Him evil for good. As He did, we can pray to God, our Father, to *"raise me up."* As long as we continue seeking Him earnestly, no enemy shall gain victory over us. "**I can do all things through Him who strengthens me.**" (Philippians 4:13)

We are not alone in this world, even when everyone has abandoned us, Jesus is our friend. "**No longer do I call you servants, for the servant does not know what his master is doing; but I have called you friends, for all that I have heard from my Father I have made known to you.**" (John 15:15) Just like Jesus, sometimes we must persevere by ourselves. Like Him, we also have a mission to complete. We cannot permit ourselves to be defeated. Despite all circumstances, we must endure and continue the mission. Jesus will be with us all along the way. "**My grace is sufficient for you, for my power is made perfect in weakness.**" Therefore, I will boast all the more gladly about my weaknesses, so that Christ's power may rest on me. That is why, for Christ's sake, I delight in weaknesses, in insults, in hardships, in persecutions, in difficulties. For when I am weak, then I am strong."** (2 Corinthians 12:9-11)

This is our life's calling, purpose, and mission: "**Go therefore and make disciples of all the nations, baptizing them in the name of the Father and of the Son and of the Holy Spirit, teaching them to observe all things that I have commanded you; and lo, I am with you always, even to the end of the age.**" (Matthew 28:19-20)

Our God watches over us and lifts us up when we fall, so that we will not become discouraged and quit. His Holy Spirit encourages us and reminds us of our glorious destination if we persevere. "*As for me, You uphold me in my integrity, and You set me in Your presence forever.*" (verse 12)

An everlasting life of joy awaits us who cling to our Maker. The mere thought of this always excites us. With King David, thousands of years later, we also ecstatically profess, "***Blessed be the Lord, the God of Israel, from everlasting to everlasting. Amen and Amen.***" (verse 13)

This concludes Book 1 of King David's Psalms.

A Study Guide:

Hope & Healing for Hard Times
King David's Psalms

Book 1

The Psalms are full of Christ. When Jesus went to the mountain to pray, David give us His prayer. The Gospels tell us that He was crucified, but the Psalms tell us the anguish in His own heart as he hung upon the cross. It is through David's very intimate relationship with Christ that we our brought into such a relationship too, by the reading and study of his Psalms.

David was a sinner, like all men, but he had a humble, servant's heart, perhaps formed from his days as a shepherd boy. His love for God was profound and a very living influence throughout his life. David was also a prophet that was given amazing and detailed insight about the future, especially the ministry of the Son of God, Jesus Christ. But what God loved the most about David was his heart, "**The LORD hath sought him a man after his own heart, and the LORD hath commanded him to be captain over his people**." (1 Samuel 13:14)

As we listen to David's praise and cries to God, they reveal our joys, strength, struggles, afflictions, and sorrows too. The strength David finds in his faith can be ours as well. As he overcomes his trials, we discover in his words and wisdom how to become victors in our life also. – It is my fervent prayer that in this book you will find, as did David, hope, and healing for hard times.

PSALM 1

1. Describe the character and behavior of the two different people that David talks about in this Psalm.
2. What do the "***blessed***" practice and not practice? (verses 1-3)

3. What do the wicked do that will cause them to be judged? (verses 4-5)

4. What does it mean to "***meditate on His word day and night?***"

6. How can our "***tree***" stay "***green***" throughout every season?

Psalm 2

1. Can you identify with hearing this in your heart? "***Break His chains. Throw off His shackles!***" Probably so, because all believers are engaged in a spiritual battle against dark forces that urge us to do so. Have you shared this with another believer? Do so now. Where are your weak spots that you need prayer for more strength?

2. Share an experience with others that ensures you that Jesus loves you and that you can trust him? What causes you to "***Kiss the Son***"?

3. When the Father installs his "***King on Zion.***" How do you picture that in your mind? Eventhough the bible says God's rule on earth is impossible for us to comprehend how beautiful and wonderful it will be, we all still dream about it. Share your vison of living together with Jesus in his holy city when He returns.

4. What does this verse mean to you? "***Serve the Lord with fear.***" (verse 11) How does our knowledge of God's love for us coincide with "fearing" the Lord?

Psalm 3

1. "***But you, Lord, are a shield around me, my glory, the One who lifts my head high.***" (verse 3) Recall and share 3 victories the Lord has given you.

2. "*I call out to the LORD, and he answers me from his holy mountain.*" – Share a "**foe**" you struggled against today. – Pray for eachother, and then hug, imagining that it is the warm, loving embrace of Jesus.

3. "*From the LORD comes deliverance.*" (verse 8A) David states this Psalm's theme in his final verse. In everything, we are to trust in the Lord, especially when *assailed by* "*foes.*" He is our refuge and our peace. – But David concludes with a prayer for others besides himself. "*May your blessing be on your people.*" (verse 8) – Each group member share about a person you know who needs prayer. Ask for the Lord to show that person His deliverance and for their eyes to see that it was the Lord who did it. May they join you in receiving Jesus Christ and also receive eternal life.

PSALM 4

1. This psalm asks us to "*search our hearts.*" What does that mean to you? And how do you do that?

2. In what ways do you "*offer the sacrifices of the righteous*?"

3. "*May your blessing be on your people.*" Think of something to do for someone in need. Bless them in secret. Do not let them know it was you. "**But when you give to the needy, do not let your left hand know what your right hand is doing, so that your giving may be in secret. Then your Father, who sees what is done in secret, will reward you.**" (Matthew 6:3-4)

4. Share a personal experience that you've had that despite "*how many rise up against you,*" you were able to "*lie down*

and sleep in peace, for you alone, LORD, make me dwell in safety." (verse 8)

5. Our blessings and answers to prayer should be recorded. Keep a journal, especially for particularly amazing blessings of God's providence. Write prayers, songs, poems, or letters to the Lord. Thanking Him for all he does for us. So that when trials, persecution, tribulations, afflictions, and broken hearts crush us, by reading these recorded testimonies, our Hope in God continues to give us strength and the confidence to not be afraid, and to continue in righteousness, until the Lord provides again.

PSALM 5

1. Do you have a set time when you privately come before the Lord? If not. Please commit yourself to a time every day to do so. For those of you who practice doing so, share when you do, and how it as affected your daily life.

2. "*Many are saying of me, "God will not deliver him."* (verse 2) We all struggle with arrogance. We all are born with a selfish spirit. That is why babies cry. We want our needs met now. Therefore, the Holy Spirit seeks to transform us into humble people who seek good for others before ourselves. – Where in your life do you struggle with pride? – Pray for eachother after each has shared.

3. David claims what all believers profess. We are saved by God's grace, not by our deeds. "*But I, by your great love, can come into your house.*" (verse 7) It is much like the Apostle Paul who

says, "**Do you not realize that it is the kindness of god that has led you to repentance.**" (Romans 2:4) –How has the love and kindness of God led you into a deeper relation with the Lord?

Psalm 6

1. How can you identify with David's conviction and sorrow over his sins? How were you reconciled with the Lord?

2. How can we be assured that if we confess our sins that God will forgive us and remember them no more? Have a group prayer in a circle. Ask the Father, in Jesus' name, to pour down a washing away of all the sins that plague us. Feel the love of God's Holy Spirit holding you together and immersing you with mercy and forgiveness. Then turn to eachother and proclaim "Your sins are washed away and remembered no more. You are forgiven, in Jesus' name!"

Psalm 7

1. When we go through trials and persecution can we also say, "***Vindicate me, Lord, according to my righteousness, according to my integrity, O Most High.***" (verse 8) What "***righteousness***" and "***integrity***" to all believers have?

2. Have we ever repaid someone with evil without cause, like David's pursuer? When we read of others' sins, always inspect ourselves before judging and ask, "Am I also guilty of this sin?" We cannot hide from God. He already knows. So, always be ready to confess our sins to God. He promises to forgive when we do. Admitting our faults to others is good for us and for

them. We all sin. That is why we come to Jesus. "**Be kind to one another, tender-hearted, *forgiving each other*, just as God in Christ also has forgiven you**." (Ephesians 4:32) – "**Therefore confess your sins to each other and pray for each other so that you may be healed**." (James 5:16) – Is there a sin or a faulty personality trait that you struggle with that you can share and receive forgiveness from God and members of your group?

3. In the middle of this psalm, we hear David's urgent plea for God to come and reign on earth in order to put an end to evil. "***Put an end to the evil of the wicked, but establish the righteous, O righteous God who searches hearts and minds***." (verse 9) – What does it make you feel like when you imagine Christ's reign on earth? Does this Great Hope give you strength to endure troubles? Read Titus 2:13-14.

Psalm 8

1. What makes you say, "Thank You, Jesus!" when you go outside on a beautiful day? Find something that especially makes you wonder at the creativity of our Maker: flowers, grass, water, trees, birds, sky, stars, etc. Share why.

Exercise: Try blindfolding eachother alternately and then leading them by hand to use their smell, hearing and touch to experience God's nature, like grass and trees and flowers and the sun without sight. Do not tell the blindfolded person what you are having them touch. Let them tell you. – This is meant to heighten our appreciation of the beauty made for us by our loving God.

2. What was the best vacation that you have taken? What effect did have on you? Were you able to relax and see more reasons to enjoy the life and the beauty God has given us? Share.

3. Share 3 things you are especially thankful to God for giving you each day. Consider how many other things that we never notice that we are blessed with every day.

Psalm 9

1. *"Endless ruin has overtaken my enemies. You have uprooted their cities; even the memory of them has perished."* (verse 6) Has this been true in your personal life since walking with the Lord? Can you share an example?

2. *"The Lord is a refuge for the oppressed, a stronghold in times of trouble."* (verse 9) How is our Lord a refuge and a stronghold when we are oppressed? When you and your loved ones experience hardships, how does your faith keep you going?

3. Who outside of your group can you choose to bless secretly? What is a need your group can meet for them? – Do you believe that your group's good deed is God using you? If so, rejoice and praise Him together for doing so. Ask Him to direct you to another person in need to secretly bless, in Jesus' name.

Psalm 10

1. Is there any difference between the way the poor and the more affluent are treated in your church? How about in the local schools, or in your community? – What can your group

do to become involved and to right the wrongs around you on behalf of the poor? – Read Deuteronomy 15:7-11.

2. As we help others, how do we share our Christian testimony at the same time, without it seeming that is the only reason we are helping them? Or is it enough of a testimony just to help them? What would Jesus do?

3. Jesus said, "**No one can serve two masters, for either he will hate the one and love the other, or he will be devoted to the one and despise the other. You cannot serve God and money.**" (Matthew 6:24) How do we not serve money in this expensive, materialistic, technological, modern world where the price of everything goes up while our earnings do not. How do we prevent ourselves from becoming like this? "*In his pride the wicked man does not seek him; in all his thoughts there is no room for God.*" (verse 4)

4. If many of the wealthy are in danger of not entering the kingdom of God, how can we reach out to them? What is the message we can share?

Psalm 11

1. *When "the wicked bend their bows"* at you, and *"set their arrows against the strings to shoot from the shadows"* at you, *"the upright in heart,"* what is your response? Do you react with angry and violent words and ways? If so, what can you do to respond with love, instead?

2. "*In the Lord I take refuge.*" (verse 1) What is your personal experience when you run to the Lord for refuge. Share an example.

3. What Godly "*foundations*" can your group help to strengthen in your community?

Psalm 12

1. As it was in David's times, so it is in ours, "*No one is faithful anymore.*" (verse 1) "*Everyone lies to their neighbor. They flatter with their lips but harbor deception in their hearts.*" (verse 2) When asked about the signs of the last days just before the reign of the Messiah begins, Jesus replied, "**Because of the increase of wickedness, the love of most will grow cold, but the one who stands firm to the end will be saved**." (Matthew 24:12-13) This will be a great opportunity for believers to shine brightly in the darkness. – What can we do to maintain our fellowship together, as God fearing people who practice integrity and honesty? How do we "*stand firm*" in the midst of a crumbling world?

2. "*Because the poor are plundered and the needy groan, I will now arise,*" *says the* Lord. "*I will protect them from those who malign them.*" (verse 5) How dangerous for us to ignore the poor, needy, and afflicted, especially within our own church. – Beware of hardening your hearts to the poor. Overlook their hardships and afflictions. Love them. We never know if and when this may happen to us also. If it were to happen. Losing everything you possess. How would you react? What would you do? Would your friends help? How would your faith sustain you?

3. "*The words of the* Lord *are flawless, like silver purified in a crucible, like gold refined seven times.*" (verse 6) Do you expe-

rience the immense worth of God's words? Does your soul thirst for them? If so, why? If not, why? What can we do to stay thirsty?

4. Pray for those you know who are struggling with poverty. Is there a 'food ministry' in your church? If so, volunteer and get to know how dear these poor Christians are. Start a food ministry in your church. Start a bible group for them. Consider having your church purchase property where poor Christians can park their cars and sleep in them at night, safely.

Psalm 13

1. Share an experience when you have had to hold on like this. How did you get through it?

2. Pray for eachother's enduring faith and love for God and others, one by one, with the laying on of hands.

3. Pray for those Christians around the world, who might also be struggling to hold on to Christ too, in the midst of trials.

Psalm 14

1. "*The fool says in his heart, "There is no God.*" (verse 1) In what ways do we express our lack of faith in God's love and concern for us when we go through trials that stretch our endurance? What does Satan, our enemy, whisper to us during these times? How do we respond?

2. "*You evildoers frustrate the plans of the poor, but the Lord is their refuge.*" (verse 6) Why does David concern himself so much with the "*poor*" and how they are treated?

3. "*Oh, that salvation for Israel would come out of Zion! When the Lord restores his people, let Jacob rejoice and Israel be glad!*" (verse 7) Why is the return of Jesus called the "**Blessed Hope?**" Read Titus 2:12-14

Psalm 15

1. "*Who may live on your holy mountain? The one whose walk is blameless, who does what is righteous, who speaks the truth from their heart; whose tongue utters no slander.*" (verses 1b-3a) What we say can save us or condemn us. "**The tongue also is a fire, a world of evil among the parts of the body. It corrupts the whole body, sets the whole course of one's life on fire, and is itself set on fire by hell.**" (James 3:6) Yet it is the most difficult of all our body members to control. "**No human being can tame the tongue. It is a restless evil, full of deadly poison.**" (James 3:8) – Have a group prayer for God to forgive the misuse of our tongues and to sanctify them for His use.

2. How is it possible for us to love our enemies? Are we capable of doing this? "**If someone slaps you on one cheek, turn to them the other also.**" (Luke 6:29) – How does being "born again" make this possible? – Discuss.

3. "*Whoever does these things will never be shaken.*" (verse 5) Each member of the group share how they remain close to the Lord. How do we "abide in Him and bear much fruit"? (John 15:5) What is our daily practice? Or what should it be? Do we have a set time every day to spend privately with Jesus? Is that time more important than anything else in our life? Why?

Psalm 16

1. "*Keep me safe, my God, for in you I take refuge.*" (verse 1) Is this all that anyone needs to plead to be saved?

2. Share your blessings. Why can you also declare, "*The boundary lines have fallen for me in pleasant places; surely I have a delightful inheritance.*" (verse 6)

3. What do imagine will happen after you die? Who do you want to see after Jesus? Describe the colors, what you smell and touch, and your emotions. "*You will not abandon me to the realm of the dead, nor will you let your faithful one see decay. You make known to me the path of life; you will fill me with joy in your presence, with eternal pleasures at your right hand.*" (verse 10-11)

Psalm 17

1. "*Keep me as the apple of your eye; hide me in the shadow of your wings.*" (verse 8) How have you experienced the comfort of finding refuge beneath God's wings? Do you walk through each day knowing that you are the "*apple*" of God's eye? What does "*the apple of my eye*" mean?

2. "*They close up their callous hearts, and their mouths speak with arrogance.*" (verse 10) When have we experienced having a "callous heart"? What is the cure?

3. "*As for me, I will be vindicated and will see your face; when I awake, I will be satisfied with seeing your likeness.*" (verse 15) Since David is a sinner, as we all are, how was he, and how are we, "*vindicated*"?

Psalm 18

1. "*I love you, Lord, my strength… who is worthy of praise.*" (verse 1&3) Why do you *love* and *praise* the Lord? Share three reasons.

2. When we go through hard times it is sometimes difficult to always believe this: "***In my distress I called to the Lord; I cried to my God for help. From his temple he heard my voice; my cry came before him, into his ears.***" (verse 6) How can we trust in God when it seems impossible for Him to help us? (See Matthew 19:26) "***He made darkness his covering, his canopy around him.***" (verse 11) In a time of *darkness*, how did the Lord "***keep your lamp burning?***" (verse 28)

3. "***I have been blameless before him and have kept myself from sin.***" (verse 23) How does David say that we can be "*blameless*" and keep ourselves from sin?

4. "***As for God, his way is perfect: The Lord's word is flawless; he shields all who take refuge in him.***" (verse 30) We trust in God because we know He is "*perfect*" and *flawless.*" Sometimes it seems impossible for this to be true. How do you persevere when you do not understand why God allows bad things to happen?

5. "***You exalted me above my foes; from a violent man you rescued me. Therefore, I will praise you, Lord, among the nations; I will sing the praises of your name.***" (verses 48-49) What have been the "***foes***" we have fought against in our personal life? And who is the "***violent man***" from whom God has rescued us?

Psalm 19

1. "*In the heavens God has pitched a tent for the sun... It rises at one end of the heavens and makes its circuit to the other; nothing is deprived of its warmth.*" (verses 5-6) – Compare the first stanza of this psalm with Matthew 5:45-46, "**But I tell you, love your enemies and pray for those who persecute you, that you may be sons of your Father in heaven. He causes His sun to rise on the evil and the good and sends rain on the righteous and unrighteous. If you love those who love you, what reward will you get? Do not even tax collectors do the same?**" – Can we, do we, love everyone upon whom the "sun rises" and those who do not love us? How?

2. Why are the "*testimonies of the Lord more precious than gold*" and "*sweeter than honey?*" (verse 10) How has this proven to be true to you?

3. "*But who can discern their own errors? Forgive my hidden faults. Keep your servant also from willful sins; may they not rule over me.*" (verses 12-13) Has the Lord ever given you a glimpse of your sinfulness, and of all the sins we commit, even just in our attitude toward others? Does it overwhelm you with guilt? Or does it bring praise to your mouth for his abundant forgiveness?

Psalm 20

1. "*May he give you the desire of your heart and make all your plans succeed.*" (verse 4) Share a testimony of how God has done this for you. Or share the desire of your heart that you are waiting for the Lord to give you.

2. "*Some trust in chariots and some in horses, but we trust in the name of the* LORD *our God.*" (verse 7) What are some things that people (and ourselves) put their trust in other than the Lord? Why is this futile?

3. What encouragement does this psalm gives we who are in distress and need to persevere?

Psalm 21

1. As you read the Psalms, do you see how David is sometimes referring to himself as the "king," and sometimes to Jesus? Discuss.

2. Do you agree that such verses as this apply to you too? "*You have bestowed on him splendor and majesty. Surely you have granted him unending blessings and made him glad with the joy of your presence.*" (verse 6) Discuss.

3. "*Your hand will lay hold on all your enemies; your right hand will seize your foes. When you appear for battle, you will burn them up as in a blazing furnace.* (verses 8-9) – Why does not David depend on the strength of his armies and his own wisdom to defeat his enemies? Who or what do we depend on when faced with great difficulties? (Be honest.)

4. How does it make you feel when you read about the destruction of the earth and the how only a few will be left alive? "**The earth is defiled by its people; they have transgressed the laws; they have overstepped the decrees and broken the everlasting covenant. Therefore, a curse has consumed the earth, and its inhabitants must bear the guilt; the earth's**

dwellers have been burned up, and only a few survive." (Isaiah 24:5-6) Explain how and why it makes you feel?

Psalm 22

1. Do you have times in your life when you have also cried out, "**Lord, why have you forsaken me?**" (verse 1) What do you do to get through until God answers?

2. "*In you our ancestors put their trust; they trusted, and you delivered them. To you they cried out and were saved; in you they trusted and were not put to shame.*" (verses 4-5) – How have your family and relatives affected your faith? – Share.

3. "*Yet you brought me out of the womb; you made me trust in you, even at my mother's breast. From birth I was cast on you; from my mother's womb you have been my God.*" (verses 9-10) – When did you come to know God? – Share your brief testimony.

4. "*Do not be far from me, for trouble is near and there is no one to help.*" (verse 11) Have you ever felt frightened and all alone with no one to help you? (I think all of us have.) How did your faith give you courage and make you aware of God's presence with you?

Psalm 23

1. To whom in your life do you also feel like a Shepherd? Who has been yours?

2. How important is it for us to experience this kind of Shepherd's love from God and from eachother?

3. How do you know positively that God exists? What has He done that is proof of His existence in your life? How do you know that Jesus Christ is the Messiah, the everlasting king to come?

4. Why is it so important for us to share God's love with others? Who can you think of who needs you to show them the love of God by listening, a hug, or an action?

5. Is it possible that if you read this tiny diamond of a psalm to an unbelieving person, and softly shared how you have experienced this Shepherd's love, that they might pray with you to become a born again child of God? Please pray about this. If you are afraid, then ask God for courage. Just share in His Holy Spirit of love and forgiveness.

Psalm 24

1. David asks the most important question that can be asked, "***Who may ascend the mountain of the Lord? Who may stand in his holy place?***" (verse 3) His answer includes four things a believer does. What are they, and how do we apply them in our lives?

2. Many verses in the Bible can have a literal and a metaphorical meaning. What else could the psalmist be asking us to lift up when he writes "***Lift up your heads, you gates; be lifted up, you ancient doors, that the King of glory may come in.***" (verse 7)

3. Take a few minutes to meditate on the meaning of "***Lord Almighty… the King of Glory***" and how it applies to your walk with the Lord.

4. Sing a song in praise of God, perhaps "Joy to the World." As you do so, imagine Jesus coming through the gates of Jerusalem and establishing his Kingdom on earth.

5. "*They will receive blessing from the L*ORD *and vindication from God their Savior. Such is the generation of those who seek him, who seek your face, God of Jacob.*" (verses 5-6) What does it mean to "*seek your face*"? How do we do that?

Psalm 25

1. "*In you, L*ORD *my God, I put my trust.*" (verse 1) Does this sum up all that we are asked to do in order to receive salvation? What else would you add to this?

2. When David says, "*teach me your paths,*" (verse 4) what does he mean? What are the Paths of the Lord?

3. "*Do not remember the sins of my youth and my rebellious ways.*" (verse 7) What are the trials and temptations of youth that lead many into rebellion against God and his ways?

4. "*Good and upright is the L*ORD*; therefore, he instructs sinners in his ways.*" (verse 8) How does the Lord "*instruct*" us when we sin?

5. "*For the sake of your name, L*ORD*, forgive my iniquity, though it is great.*" (verse 11) Why is the honor of God's name at stake when we ask Him to forgive us?

6. How do you manifest "*integrity and uprightness*" (verse 21) *in your life?*

Psalm 26

1. Since no one is "***blameless***" of sinning, what does David mean when he says, "***I have led a blameless life***"? How does this apply to us and our salvation?

2. When David asks the Lord to "***examine my heart and my mind,***" (verse 2) what is he asking the Lord to find?

3. "***My feet stand on level ground.***" (verse 12) List the things in this psalm David claims he does that enables him to be able to make this claim.

Psalm 27

1. "***The Lord is my light and my salvation– whom shall I fear?***" (verse 1) In what ways is God a "***light***" in your life?

2. What is the, "***One thing I ask from the Lord, this only do I seek.***" (verse 4)

3. "***For in the day of trouble he will keep me safe in his dwelling; he will hide me in the shelter of his sacred tent and set me high upon a rock.***" (verse 5) How do we react when we do not put out trust in Lord "***in the day of trouble.***" What is the meaning of "***He…set me upon a rock?***"

4. In what circumstances do you hear this in your heart most often? My heart says of you, "***Seek his face!***" (verse 8)

5. Personally, this tiny verse is one that has helped me throughout my life. How does this verse relate to you in your life? "***Wait for the Lord; be strong and take heart and wait for the Lord.***" (verse 14)

Psalm 28

1. "*To you, Lord, I call; you are my Rock, do not turn a deaf ear to me. For if you remain silent, I will be like those who go down to the pit.*" (verse 1) Can you identify with David being at the end of his rope? How do you respond after praying, when it seems that God has turned "*a deaf ear*" to you? (verse 1) Does our Savior ever turn a deaf ear to us? – Share a circumstance and how, after waiting, God has responded to that prayer.

2. David often says that while praying he "*lifts his hands.*" (verse 2) How do you feel about doing this? Do you think it helps? Why?

3. The Bible warns us about being those who "*speak cordially with their neighbors but harbor malice in their hearts.*" (verse 3) How should we respond to bad neighbors when they offend us?

5. Pray this prayer of David for your church and Christian friends. "*Save your people and bless your inheritance; be their shepherd and carry them forever.*" (verse 9)

Psalm 29

1. When sudden emergencies happen in your life, how do you react? Are you able to stay calm, or do you become distracted with fear? How does your faith enter into these dire circumstances?

2. How responsible is God for what happens to you? What has He promised to do for us when we are afraid? (Deuteronomy 31:8, Romans 8:28, Isaiah 43:1, Psalm 18:2)

Psalm 30

1. "*For his anger lasts only a moment, but his favor lasts a lifetime.*" (verse 5) How has God's anger expressed itself when we stray from the straight and narrow path?

2. What do we do when we need to repent and get back on the right way? See verses 2-4. What three steps happened between David and God when he called for help?

3. "*When I felt secure, I said, "I will never be shaken… you hid your face, I was dismayed.*" (verses 6-7) – Can we ever be too confident in our relationship with God? Why did God hide his face?

4. "*What is gained if I am silenced, if I go down to the pit? Will the dust praise you? Will it proclaim your faithfulness?*" (verse 9) Can we say this about ourselves to the Lord? Are we always declaring the goodness of the Lord and praising Him?

5. "*LORD my God, I will praise you forever.*" (verse 12) Life is not a bed of roses for anyone. It is filled with hardships in many ways. How can we continue to praise our Lord in the midst of daily tribulations and trials?

Psalm 31

1. "*In you, LORD, I have taken refuge; let me never be put to shame; deliver me in your righteousness.*" (verse 1) How are we delivered "*in your (God's) "righteousness"*?

2. "*How abundant are the good things that you have stored up for those who fear you, that you bestow in the sight of all,*

on those who take refuge in you." (verse 19) Does taking time to read scripture, meditate on it, and pray before beginning our days, help us to walk in the Spirit?

3. How often do we converse with God? – Never? Occasionally? Just in time of trouble? Constantly?

4. Have you ever felt like this? "*I am the utter contempt of my neighbors and an object of dread to my closest friends.*" (verse 11) Of course, rejection and loneliness hurt deeply. How does knowing God help you through these times?

Psalm 32

1. How do we interpret this as it applies to ourselves? "*in whose spirit is no deceit.*" (verse 1) How are we *deceitful* towards others? And how are others deceitful to us?

2. Can we identify with David's feelings before he confessed? "*When I kept silent, my bones wasted away through my groaning all day long… my strength was sapped as in the heat of summer.*" (verse 4) What do we experience that leads us to repent?

3, What do you think? If a person who never got a real opportunity to know Jesus Christ by name does as David does here, are they also saved? "*Then I acknowledged my sin to you and did not cover up my iniquity. I said, "I will confess my transgressions to the Lord." And you forgave the guilt of my sin.*" (verse 5)

4. What are the different ways that God teaches and counsels us? "*I will instruct you and teach you in the way you should go; I will counsel you with my loving eye on you.*" (verse 8)

Psalm 33

1. Frequently, David instructs us to praise the Lord with singing. Share some favorite songs you sing to the Lord. Then choose a song all know and sing together.

1. Do you have times in your life when you have also cried out, when God's "***hand was heavy on me; my strength was sapped as in the heat of summer.***" (verse 4) What should we do when that happens? – See verse 5.

2. "***In you our ancestors put their trust; they trusted, and you delivered them. To you they cried out and were saved; in you they trusted and were not put to shame.***" (verses 4-5) – How have your family and relatives affected your faith? – Share.

3. "***Yet you brought me out of the womb; you made me trust in you, even at my mother's breast. From birth I was cast on you; from my mother's womb you have been my God.***" – When did you come to know God? – Share your brief testimony.

4. "***The word of the Lord is right and true; he is faithful in all he does.***" (verse 4) Since we are to trust in the Lord, and lean not on our own understanding, what do we do when science disagrees, as with the seven days of creation?

5. What does this verse mean to you? Discuss. "***Blessed is the nation whose God is the Lord, the people he chose for his inheritance.***" (verse 12)

6. David says that our God is "***he who forms the hearts of all.***" (verse 15) What does this mean? Does he form them at our birth; or is it saying that God is forming our hearts; or both?

Psalm 34

1. "*I will extol the LORD at all times; his praise will always be on my lips.*" (verse 1) David claims to praise the Lord continuously, in all circumstances. Is this really possible?

2. Who do you think the "*afflicted*" (verse 2) are? Would they be the homeless, the physically and mentally ill? Who else?

3. What does it mean to be "*covered with shame*"? (verse 5)

4. What does it mean to "*fear the Lord*"? (verse 9)

5. Who are the "*crushed*" and "*broken hearted*" (verse 18) that you know? How can you strengthen and encourage them?

6. This is perhaps the most important verse in this psalm, "*No one who takes refuge in him will be condemned.*" (verse 22) Discuss.

Psalm 35

1. Have you also suffered from being despised by those you love? How did this feel? How did you respond? How did your faith help?

2. How does God heal our broken hearts? Or does he? Jesus died from a broken heart. Will some healing not take place until we are with Jesus?

3. How did David, and how can we rejoice and sing "**praises all day long,**" (verse 28) when we are heartbroken? What do we praise God for?

Psalm 36

1. "*In their own eyes they flatter themselves too much to detect or hate their sin.*" (verse 2) How do we witness to such people? Or can we?

2. "*Your love, Lord, reaches to the heavens, your faithfulness to the skies.*" (verse 5) Share an example of why you know this to be true.

3. Discuss this verse and its meaning to you and others. "*For with you is the fountain of life; in your light we see light.*" (verse 9)

Psalm 37

1. It seems to be innate for most humans to crave ease and comfort, and to escape the curse upon mankind that began with Adam and Eve. "*By the sweat of your brow you will eat your food until you return to the ground.*" (Genesis 3:19) How can we not be envious of those who live in comfort and luxury?

2. "*Take delight in the Lord, and he will give you the desires of your heart.*" (verse 4) What are the things that your hearts desires?

3. "*Be still before the Lord.*" (verse 7) What does this mean? How is it done?

4. "*Refrain from anger and turn from wrath; do not fret – it leads only to evil.*" (verse 8) In the verse that follows this, (verse 9), what are the consequences if we do not obey this?

5. This was written 3,000 years ago. "*A little while, and the wicked will be no more; though you look for them, they will not be found.*" (verse 10) When will this day come?

6. Why is it so important, as confessing Christians, that we repay our debts and give to those in more need than ourselves? "*The wicked borrow and do not repay, but the righteous give generously.*" (verse 21) – See verse 25

7) When God speaks of our "future," what do you imagine? "*a future awaits those who seek peace.*" (verse 37)

Psalm 38

1. "*Lord, do not rebuke me in your anger or discipline me in your wrath.*" (verse 1) Despite God's constant loving care for us, why do we still sin?

2. What does it feel like when we hide our sins and do not confess? – Verses 2-14

3. Will God always forgive us if we repent? What if we continue to struggle with those sins, does he give up on us? Read 1 John 1:9.

Psalm 39

1. Can we identify with this psalm? Have we ever also felt rejected by God because of our sins?

2. Regarding David's reference about how brief our lives are, about what age do you think David was when he wrote this? Young or Old? When do we begin thinking about the brevity of our life?

4. In verse 7 David asks, "***But now, Lord, what do I look for?***" Above all else what do you desire from God?

5. "***When you rebuke and discipline anyone for their sin, you consume their wealth like a moth.***" (verse 11) Is this more often true for believers than unbelievers? Why?

6. What does it mean when David refers to himself as this? "***I dwell with you as a foreigner, a stranger, as all my ancestors were.***" (verse 12) How are we also foreigners and strangers? Read John 17:16.

Psalm 40

1. Can we identify with the painful experience and then exhilaration of what David has gone through? Crushed by guilt and depression, and then having our joy restored by the Lord?

2. "***He put a new song in my mouth, a hymn of praise to our God. Many will see and fear the Lord and put their trust in him.***" (verse 3) David's personal experience of confessing his sins humbly, and then receiving God's forgiveness is his testimony that he has shared. As a result, of doing so what does he predict will happen?

3. There seems to be a natural response to for many people to admire proud and arrogant leaders. However, we are warned, "***Blessed is the one who trusts in the Lord, who does not look to the proud, to those who turn aside to false gods.***" (verse 4) Define "*false gods*" as used in this verse. How should Godly leaders be, instead?

4. "*Sacrifice and offering you did not desire – but my ears you have opened – burnt offerings and sin offerings you did not require.*" (verse 6) What does the Lord desire more than sacrifice? Read Hosea 6:6.

5. How does this verse apply to us and all believers? "*I do not hide your righteousness in my heart; I speak of your faithfulness and your saving help. I do not conceal your love and your faithfulness from the great assembly.*" (verse 10)

Psalm 41

1. "*Blessed are those who have regard for the weak.*" (verse 1) David uses several key phrases in his first stanza to define his meaning of the "*weak.*" God "*delivers them in times of trouble… does not give them over to the desire of their foes… restores them from their bed of illness.*" (verses 1-3)

2. David admits that his weakness is due to a sin he has committed, "*Have mercy on me, Lord; heal me, for I have sinned against you.*" (verse 4) Is all sickness due to sin? Can a believer honestly answer "yes," and "no?" Reference John 9:1-6 and Romans 5:12.

3. "*Even my close friend, someone I trusted, one who shared my bread, has turned against me.*" (verse 9) This happened to David, and the "Son of David," the Lord Jesus Christ. Unfortunately, almost all of us can identify with the anguish they both felt. – Does it help us to know when we are heartbroken that Jesus knows that feeling too?

4. "***Because of my integrity you uphold me and set me in your presence forever.***" (verse 12) What is the "*integrity*" that believers possess that uphold us and sets us in God's presence forever?

About The Author

Mark Baird has been preaching the Word of God for more than 50 years. He is married to Tori Baird. They have been blessed to have been given the ministry of helping others. Most specifically, they serve US veterans and their families. They have put many thousands of US veterans to work via their unique Hire Patriots program. They also created Horses 4 Healing Heroes, an equine therapy center, especially for veterans, first responders, doctors, nurses, and police. They host 3-day, all expenses paid, marriage retreats for them. And they have assisted in creating over 100 veterans owned businesses.

US Presidents, Congress, and municipalities have awarded them. They have appeared on various national News programs, and PEOPLE magazine selected them as their Heroes Among Us. Patriotic Hearts their charity.

Mark and Tori share their faith by doing good for others. They believe that by building such relationships it opens peoples' hearts to listening to the Good News.

If you have a church or organization that needs a revival of excitement, gratitude and praise for our wonderful Maker, Savior and King to come, reach-out and schedule a visit from them.

Made in the USA
Middletown, DE
12 August 2023

36477499R00146